"In brilliant allegorical fashion reminiscent of John Bunyan's *Pilgrim's Progress,* David Trementozzi, in *The Way of the Thorn*, squarely faces one of life's central dilemmas: suffering. Drawing on the imagery of Paul's 'thorn in the flesh,' Trementozzi masterfully weaves a tale that not only brings understanding, but elicits hope and centers us once again on the joy and peace that caresses the soul whose aim is to be made like Jesus."

Steve Fry, Founder/Director of Messenger Fellowship

"David Trementozzi has gifted us with an extraordinary message in *The Way of The Thorn*. He delicately works his way through deep issues of the heart and offers us a look into a true mirror, if we dare. Without condemnation, he calls us to love courageously on a level of awareness of self and God that we don't step into very often. His words will call you to return to the beginning to find your way to the future."

Robert Stearns, Founder/Director of Eagles' Wings

"In *The Way of the Thorn,* David reveals many of the obstacles and faulty mindsets prevalent among believers today that keep them from achieving greater levels of spiritual maturity and ultimately their destinies in God. The truths in this story will help to bring clarity to your journey in God and rekindle a fresh fire of increased consecration and passion for God."

Larry Kreider, Director of Dove Christian Fellowship Int'l

"In *The Way of the Thorn*, David Trementozzi has captured in a beautiful way the journey of the soul, dealing with such issues as pain and injury, hiding and hypocrisy, and ultimately leading the reader to the healing presence of Jesus as the life of God is released in the soul of man."

Jonathan Smoak, Senior Pastor, The Tabernacle Church

"Deeper levels of communion and consecration in the areas of worship and prayer are in store for those who learn to apply the truths found in *The Way of the Thorn*. I highly recommend this book for all who are longing for a breakthrough to greater depths in their relationship with God."

JoAnn McFatter, worship leader, recording artist, teacher

"*The Way of the Thorn* gives the reader a new way of understanding the Christian journey of spiritual brokenness. Trementozzi takes us through a thought provoking journey of pain and grace and of trial and faith. It is a stimulating resource for those who hunger for a deeper grasp of the Lord's ways in bringing us to a place of inner wholeness."

Dotty Schmitt, teacher, author

"David Trementozzi's passion in *The Way of the Thorn* is to reveal that much of spiritual transformation comes from a godly response to the painful times in our lives, not the 'polished' times in our programs or on our platforms. With creativity and insight, David hits the mark on a Kingdom definition of success: growth and change into Christ-likeness."

Dr. Joseph Umidi, Professor of Practical Theology, Regent University

"As you read *The Way of the Thorn,* you will find gems of God's ways revealed to you through the life of Jesus as expressed through David Trementozzi. This book is refreshing, poetic, and piercing; with clarity David writes with the pen of our Master. Read this book, and it will read you!"

Jim W. Goll, Co-founder of Ministry to the Nations

"*The Way of the Thorn* is a priceless novel for anyone, old or young, to identify with the process of being broken and remade into the best possible vessel for the Father's use. Trementozzi has captured the heart of the Maker of Life to reveal His love, discipline, and breaking power to keep us pointed toward our eternal goal. This book will comfort, console, and provide wisdom on your journey."

Chuck D. Pierce, President, Glory of Zion International Ministries

"This allegory reveals the journey of faith and the great need of everyone to traverse this path with humility and self surrender. Trementozzi helps us all to understand how to no longer fear the "thorn" we've learned to avoid, but instead to embrace it as a dear friend that is able to change our lives forever."

Roy Ellis, Senior Pastor,Christian Assembly, Madisonville, KY

"In *The Way of the Thorn,* David Trementozzi expresses profound truth in a novel way so that everyone can understand its meaning. Written in the genre of *Pilgrim's Progress*, it is entertaining, yet thought provoking. This book will surely cause soul-searching and spiritual awakening in the lives of those who read it."

Wesley Campbell, Founder, Praying the Bible Series/Revival Now!

The Way of the Thorn

David Trementozzi

The Way of the Thorn
by David Trementozzi

ISBN 1-58169-097-5
For Worldwide Distribution
Printed in the U.S.A.

Evergreen Press
P.O. Box 91011 • Mobile, AL 36691
800-367-8203

Published in cooperation with
Kairos Publishing
a division of Eagles Wings
www.eagleswings.to
www.thewayofthethorn.com

TABLE OF CONTENTS

DEDICATION

I dedicate this book to my wife Emily. I am so thankful that God has given us each other for life's journey this side of heaven. May we always be rich in faith, hope, and love so that we can embrace whatever thorns God has granted. Together may we discover the wonders of His grace. I love you Emily!

ACKNOWLEDGMENTS

If there is one lesson I have learned in writing this book, it is that book writing is a process—a back and forth process of writing and rewriting. Such a process has had a definite ebb and flow of fulfillment and challenge. Through it all I am so glad that I stuck with it.

First, I want to thank my parents, Daniel and Stephanie Trementozzi, for their undying support and encouragement to me in my writing. I want to thank my wife, Emily for believing in me and loving me in a truly remarkable way, especially in her willingness to let me take the hours I needed to complete this book.

I want to thank my friend and brother Robert Stearns and the entire Eagles' Wings family for bearing with me in the encouragement and support needed during the years of writing this book.

I also want to thank Evergreen Press for their belief in me as a writer and their confidence in the message of this book. Thank you Brian for being willing to take the risk, Keith for encouraging me to submit the story, and Kathy for your excellent editorial work and help in fine tuning this story.

Lastly, I want to thank God for giving me the story and making all of this possible. Mostly I want to thank Him for His tremendous grace of perseverance to not give up in finding the words needed to capture and develop this book into the details of its story. I am truly blessed to have had this absolutely wonderful privilege.

FOREWORD

Truly becoming a disciple of Jesus Christ is a very different thing than simply naming His name. To follow Him fully means embracing all of Him and all of His message, the glorious as well as the difficult. Even in the days of Jesus, there were times when many of His followers left Him because He was uttering "hard sayings" that caused folks to realize that the price of true discipleship was too high—one they were not willing to pay.

Accepting the "difficult" parts of following Christ without becoming morbidly introspective is also a challenge. Too many times, the message of brokenness has led to a focus merely on the deficiency of self rather than the sufficiency of Christ.

David Trementozzi has gifted the Body of Christ with an extraordinary message in *The Way of The Thorn*. He delicately works his way through deep issues of the heart and offers us a look into a true mirror... if we dare. Without condemnation or an unhealthy focus on self, he calls us to love courageously in a level of reality and awareness of self and God that we don't step into very often. His words ring true; they will strike a chord in your heart calling you to return to the beginning to find your way to the future.

David has been chosen by the Lord to share this message because he has purchased it. He has bought "gold refined in the fire" and become a vessel of honor in the house of the Lord. Like his biblical namesake, David always reminds us that the message of the Lord is very simple and focused—it is about one thing, and one desire.

I urge you to journey through this story and read it

deeply. Then read it again. Then read it with your wife and with your children. Let the Holy Spirit use the delicate instrument of this book to shape and refine your soul—pruning this, fortifying that. This book will help you become a vessel of honor, fit for the Master's use.

Shalom,
Robert Stearns
Eagles' Wings, Executive Director

INTRODUCTION

Our hearts ache for a higher quality of life; our souls hunger to know and experience the Lord of all life. Where has He gone? Why don't we see Him?

God tries to get our attention but we are perpetually restrained from His persistent beckoning by the distractions of life. When He speaks, we are often deaf because we are more in touch with other voices around us. He comes to us, but we are often blind because we are preoccupied with our busyness and the urgency of our perceived needs and oblivious to the reality of His unrelenting presence. We will never come to experience the reality of God's presence until we first face the root cause of the restlessness and distractions in our lives.

Each of us is innately born with the awareness of two divine realities. The first is the wonderful reality of God's presence and love for us. The second is the terrifying reality of life apart from the presence and love of God. Yet we are hindered in the application of both these realities. Why is this? Because we have been born with a deadly spiritual disease called sin. Sin blinds us to the reality of God's presence and love for us. And sin also blinds us to the terribly agonizing reality of estrangement from our Creator. The pain that comes when we finally understand our separation from God is so piercing that most of us have learned to ignore, deny, or downplay its reality.

So God, in the severest of mercy, has given mankind the gift of the thorn. Every day, in a multitude of ways, He allows us to know and feel the reality of our aloneness, estrangement, and isolation from Him—of such is the substance of our thorns. His desire is that the prodding and poking of this painful thorn would break through every distraction, expose every false hope, and dismantle every lie to point us towards that only which is true and secure—Himself. Without such thorns, we would remain locked in our mindsets of deceptions. We would settle into a false but comfortable sense of security that comes from the matrix of sin—a false sense of reality leading one into true peril and loss.

Are you afraid to see a glimpse of the agonizing sin nature you know is inside of you? Are you afraid to gaze upon the hope of Christ for fear that it might not be real? Jesus made provision for us that we don't have to live in bondage to fear. When we experience the honest awareness of the dismal state of our own isolated existence apart from God, we are then led to a place of desperate faith where we can truly meet God.

If we desire to live the quality of life that our hearts yearn for, then we must learn to lay hold of the virtues of ruthless honesty and fearless courage. Honesty to finally look upon our lives as they really are, no longer as we wish them to be. And courage to not only admit our human weakness and need (to be what we want and to do what we ought), but to actually embrace this painful reality as truly our own. It is only at this terribly glorious place that we discover the treasure of His presence. The terrible pain of honesty and truth releases the glorious gift of His goodness and grace so that we can experience life to the full. There we finally come to see that the agony we have always feared to face has itself paved the way for the greatest joy we could ever know.

David Trementozzi
May 2002

PROLOGUE

In the beginning, a quality of life existed on the face of the earth—its substance was glory and its perpetual effect was destiny. This was the state of our parents until that fateful day when time and space stood still, and man and woman painfully gasped at the pounding of truth's hammer into the very guts of their souls. Panic-stricken and terrified, they were now aware of something they had never felt before—*aloneness*.

Though the sovereign decree was already proclaimed and transgression's boundaries pronounced, all of this was nothing compared to the horror they now faced. The doorway was no longer open—it was guarded, secured, and forever sealed. The burning creatures had been sent with their terrible swords of fire to guard it. This side of heaven, from this point on, no man or woman would ever walk in the same communion of perfect fellowship they once had known with the Creator.

The couple clutched each other, sobbing together. They desperately sought to still the terror now permanently etched in their souls. The oneness of love they used to know flowed from the heart of their Creator into this husband and wife. Their love, His love, together was one love and could only be found in the garden where they once lived.

Looking into each other's eyes, Adam and Eve collapsed onto the ground—ground once soft and pure, now cursed and thorny. Suddenly they gripped their sides in searing pain at their newfound discovery—a wound in each of their sides, flowing with blood and burning like fire. Cursed produce of the ground had risen up, not content to infect merely the dust of the earth, but now the living dust—the dust of flesh. Flesh now had the disease as well. It too was cursed! The culprit? A thorn, now embedded in human dust, impaled in bloody flesh.

Doubled over in pain, slowly they lifted their heads upward to heaven. Their soul's horror now finally erupted as they bellowed forth, "NO-O-O-O-O-O-O!"

Thus, into the atmosphere, around earth's globe, and forward in time through every generation yet to be birthed, was released the terrifying Cry of the Thorn—the cry of mortal brokenness and an awareness of Eden's estrangement.

Now millenniums later, the story that follows is about a particular son of Adam and the journey he took to discover the glorious life that his ancestors had lost.

Have you felt the pain? Have you heard the wail? Remember the paradox, understand the mystery. The glorious journey of life is found on the terrible Way of the Thorn—the glorious path of grace.

PART I

ACCEPTING THE THORN

There was given me a thorn in my flesh, a messenger of Satan, to torment me. Three times I pleaded with the Lord to take it away from me. But he said to me, "My grace is sufficient for you, For my power is made perfect in weakness."

II CORINTHIANS 12:7-9

Chapter One

THE JOURNEY

Walking aimlessly down Center Street during his lunch hour, Jack Avery looked like the epitome of success—unless you happened to peer more closely at his face. Something there didn't quite match the snappy suit and expensive loafers that he wore.

Stopping at a storefront window in order to kill time, Jack's eyes lit up when he saw the freshly cut bouquet of exquisite roses with droplets of water still clinging to their petals. "Absolutely beautiful!" he exclaimed to no one in particular.

As he stood quietly staring at the lush, red flowers, his smile slowly faded.

Why does a beautiful flower have to endure such an ugly nuisance like thorns on its stem? he wondered. *Why did God create it that way... surely He could have left out the thorns.*

Despite his melancholic musings, the roses attracted him in a way he couldn't explain. As he entered the old-fashioned store, the little bell jingled in a friendly way.

"Hello," came the muffled voice of a man from behind the glass cases. "I'll be right with you."

Jack turned from the well-worn counter and walked over to the window display to get a closer look at the roses.

A gray-haired man finally appeared with a basket of daisies that he set on a display. "Sorry to keep you waiting. How can I help you, sir?"

"These must be the most beautiful roses I've ever seen," Jack said, turning around to face the storeowner.

The old man was slightly bent over and wore a protective apron that accentuated his protruding middle. He looked as though he had put in many years of long workdays, yet his eyes still twinkled with joy.

"I grow them myself. You are looking at the product of 50 years of experimenting. How many would you like?" he explained as he began to reach for a pair of gardening gloves.

"Oh, none today. I just came in to get a closer look. I always enjoy looking at beautiful things, and I must say that I've never seen any roses as nice as these. I will definitely be back!"

The store owner beamed. "By the way, we have a special Valentine's Day sale beginning next week."

"I'll be sure to get some then...you can count on it!" Jack said as he left the store.

Walking toward his car on the other side of the street, he mused, *Valentine's Day...already one year...* It had been one year since he first met his fiancée Julie. Engaged just three weeks ago, they were now beginning to plan their summer wedding, and he was excited although somewhat nervous.

As he opened the car door, Jack's right eye began to twitch, and an excruciating pain suddenly pierced his side. "Augggh!" wailed Jack as he violently gripped his side and just managed to collapse into the leather bucket seat.

Slow, slow, easy, breathe, breathe...that's better. Relax, breathe, relax...ok, easy, easy now. Jack coached himself through the awful recurring pain he had recently begun to experience just below his heart.

Over the last month, these sudden, dagger-like assaults in his side had sent him to the doctor. Where the pains came from, neither he nor a number of other specialists could figure out. The only diagnosis they could give him was "too much stress," and with it the old suggestion to "slow down." He had been told the same thing periodically by his parents and friends for the last two years. He could still hear their voices in his head: "Slow down, Jack. Slow down. You live like you're running from something!" Each time, these voices would trigger a mental response within him: *Running from something? You'd better believe I'm running from something. I'm running from missing life and letting it pass me by. Everybody wants to just sit around and expect life to somehow happen. Well, I know better.*

Jack hunched over the steering wheel, his knuckles turning white from gripping it so tightly. After a few minutes the pain disappeared, only to be replaced by another recurring and unwelcomed feeling—an eerie restlessness that always followed this painful experience for just a brief moment. Once the pain subsided today, however, the lingering cloud of anxiousness remained over him.

Jack looked up and stared deeply into his rearview mirror.

What's wrong with you, Jack? What's going on in there? He stared into his eyes as though trying to see something deep down in his soul. *What's wrong?*

Jack knew something in him was being unearthed, something that made him uncomfortable, and it was beginning to disrupt his life. Jack, who had always been seen as "Mr. Together," was becoming unable to effectively cope with his life.

Well liked by all those around him, Jack was especially known for his kind, well-meaning, and easy-going demeanor. After graduating from college several years ago, Jack had taken a position as a youth minister at a small church in a neighboring town close to where he had grown up. The job changed his life. During the course of the years he spent there, Jack discovered that he wanted to devote the rest of his life to serving God as a minister. Yet, in spite of this tremendous discovery, Jack began to feel a nagging weight of heaviness with increased feelings of sadness and sorrow.

The last six years of Jack's life had become intensely busy, even frantic at times. The tension build-up from his lifestyle had become so severe that two years ago it had finally taken its toll. Something inside of him broke or snapped. Jack had no idea what exactly happened, but he was certain it had to do with his soul, and he was convinced that he desperately needed help. Jack felt frustration begin to mount because no matter how much he prayed, his situation stayed the same. It seemed to him that as far as God was concerned, Jack's door of communication with Him was firmly shut.

No longer was Jack so sure of his ministerial aspirations. He took a leave of absence from his position as youth pastor and began to work as a salesman for a large insurance firm. Jack began to ignore his despondent feelings in order to appear happy and confident for his customers, co-workers, and boss. Eventually Jack became so adept at ignoring his inner war that he had nearly convinced himself that he was fine, at least until the jabbing pain began to appear. Each recurrence was a little more fierce than the last, reminding him that he was not well and that he still needed help.

To family, friends, and co-workers, his life seemed all that it should be. He had a successful job in sales, a close group of friends, a loving family, and a wonderful fiancée. Everyone looked up to Jack; he was successful on the outside but falling apart inside. Jack felt tired all day long and drank more coffee than was good for him just to keep him going at his usual pace. He had even developed a nervous stomach, so his appetite was barely what it used to be.

Jack also had a mysterious visual malady. At times, his eyes were strangely unfocused and, though he could still see, something about his vision seemed strangely out of focus. During these times, he would feel disassociated from his surroundings—physically present but emotionally absent. With this disassociation came a keen sense of despair, though Jack could never isolate the reason for it.

These problems had grown worse over the last few weeks perhaps because life had recently become even more stressful with his wedding plans and all the responsibilities that a wife and future family would represent.

Driving home after work, Jack was unable to shake this last onslaught of eerie restlessness.

Jack swerved over to the side of the road and jerked to a stop. Staring straight ahead with his hands still locked tightly on the steering wheel, he wrestled with admitting his problem. Finally as if releasing a dammed up river, he lifted his head and burst forth, "Help me, God! I'm a mess!" As he dropped his head onto the steering wheel, quiet tears began to roll. It had probably been five years since Jack last remembered shedding a tear, and that was at his grandfather's funeral.

Silence seeped into the car, and he began to feel a weight lifting.

In the strangest way, a cool, refreshing breeze began to blow over Jack, from the top of his head, over his shoulders and down his back, leaving in its wake the sensation of freedom and peace. Deep down he knew that at last the power of denial had finally been broken.

Suddenly he had an intense yearning for the outdoors. *I need space. I need air. I need the mountains.*

Inside his heart he felt a rising sense of hope. Jack felt good for the first time in weeks.

Yes, a weekend away. I'll go to the mountains. Fresh air and natural beauty. That's it, a weekend hike.

At home Jack was able to eat more than he had in awhile. Charged with excitement, he spent the evening rounding up his gear and packing supplies. He gave Julie a quick call to let her know what he was doing. She had been planning on shopping for her wedding gown with her mother, so she was not too disappointed in missing their Saturday date.

Finally he crawled into bed and surprisingly fell asleep right away. Early the next morning, with backpack and gear carefully stowed in his trunk, Jack drove off to his mountain weekend.

Not too far down the road, it happened once more. "Auggh! Not again!" Jack cried out with familiar pain as he gripped his side.

With one hand on the steering wheel, Jack determinedly kept driving down the highway.

He slowly breathed in and out, in and out, until the pain left.

I'm not improving. Oh God, help me!

Keeping his eyes focused on the road ahead, he began to force happy memories of hiking and camping into his mind. *I'm sure the fresh air and scenery will help...* Slowly the pain subsided, and Jack breathed a sigh of relief.

After three hours of uneventful driving, Jack arrived at the roadside parking lot next to the hiking trail entrance. Strapping on his backpack, Jack made his way toward the trail. Looking down at his watch, he began to determine how long the hike would take him.

Let's see it's 10:30...I think it's about 20 miles. That should bring me back here at the end of the trail's loop tomorrow afternoon about two or three. Yeah, there's the sign over there. What does it say?

He walked closer, *New Heights Trail: 25 miles... uh-h-h-h... Whoa, w-w-what's h-happening?"*

Jack's legs were suddenly weak, and his vision began to blur. He rubbed his eyes as the sign before him began to ripple in a disturbing wave-like fashion. Then the words on the sign began to squirm like white worms against a brown backdrop as they mysteriously reshaped themselves. Suddenly everything about him became foggy. Overwhelmed with dizziness, Jack fell to his hands and knees. In a few moments, the dizziness passed, and what was previously a blurry gray mass focused into a gravel pathway, and what felt like a vague discomfort on his hands and knees likewise came into focus as rocks and pebbles jabbing his kneecaps and hands. Jack gathered himself together and stood up.

Something was different...very different.

In a strange way, Jack sensed that he was standing at the crossroads of two worlds.

What's going on? This is crazy.

Chapter Two

A NEW WORLD...

Jack glanced back to the entrance of the trail. He squinted hard and rubbed his eyes trying to clear them because everything looked blurry back there, as when one is underwater, looking upward at the trees and sky. He quickly turned around and everything he saw farther up the trail was crystal clear, as though he had stepped from one world into another—from one dimension into an entirely new one.

Confused, Jack headed up the trail. After taking a few steps, he froze in his tracks with a chilling sense of ominous foreboding.

The trail sign to his right no longer read, "Welcome to New Heights Trail," rather, it now clearly read, "Welcome to the Pathway of Faith." Directly above this sign was a wooden archway spanning the width of the trail—each end connected to the top of a sturdy log post stuck firmly in the ground. The archway read, "The Journey of Honest Reckoning."

Suddenly a mighty peal of thunder cracked across

the sky. A bright ball of fiery light shot down through the tall dense trees surrounding Jack, flooding the forest with an other-worldly illumination. Slowly the light began to fade, leaving a very unusual pulsating, glowing ball of flames hovering in front of Jack.

His legs began to quiver, then shake—all of his strength suddenly drained out as he collapsed to his knees again.

In a matter of moments, the flaming mass began to change—part of it stretched upward and part downward, and then it began to widen into a flaming pillar. The flames and light faded in brilliance and began to form into the shape of a man. The being reached down and touched Jack's shoulder. Through the touch, a force was released so powerfully as to pull Jack up and onto his feet.

The next thing Jack realized was that he was standing face to face with the being.

"Wh-h-o are you?" Jack finally managed to ask.

The ground shook, thunder rumbled in the sky, and the trees rustled in the woods. The being glowed for a minute and then faded back.

"I am Azarel."

Wide eyed, Jack stuttered, "W-w-where d-d-did you c-c-come f-f-f-from?"

"I was sent. Do not fear."

"Who sent you?"

Azarel paused, looked deep into Jack's eyes, first into the place called a soul, then even deeper into that sacred place the ancients called "spirit."

He then announced, "LIFE. Life Himself has sent me. The One Who is, was, and always will be. This is the One Who fashioned and formed you. This One is called, 'God' and 'Father,' this One has sent me."

"The Father?" Jack whispered.

"Yes, He is also known as Lord, Creator, and Father King. The grandeur of His being supersedes any human attempts to contain Him in a single word, so He has many names. On this journey He shall be known as the Father King."

"W-w-what j-j-journey?"

"Jack, you are about to begin the most significant journey you have ever taken. On this journey, the Father King wants you to see life as it really is, and no longer as you wish it to be. This Journey of Honest Reckoning will bring healing for your soul. Because the Father loves you so much and has seen your soul's anguish, He has summoned me to be your guide on the journey. It is my purpose to help you and to lead you along the way. I was sent on your behalf—my name, Azarel, means God's help."

Jack was utterly dumfounded. All he could do was stare at Azarel as his mind tried to take in the bizarre events playing out before him.

"Where will this journey take me?"

"On the Journey of Honest Reckoning, one is never told exactly *where one is going*, except that it will be to a better place. The more important issue is *how one will go*. You can only proceed in faith, Jack. Look down at the ground. What do you see?"

"I see a gray gravel path."

"Lift your vision higher."

Jack raised his head and looked farther down the path. "I see a red-bricked pathway connected to it."

Jack followed Azarel forward until they were standing in front of the red path.

"What you see here, Jack, is more than a red-bricked

pathway. What you see is the Pathway of Faith. By this pathway alone will you be brought to your destination. As long as you stay on it, you *will* arrive. There are many other connecting pathways and trails you will see along the way that are unnecessary detours. You must especially beware of the Trails of Intellect and the Trails of Emotion. Never forget that it is faith's road alone that will bring you to the journey's end. Your job and your choice is to steadfastly remain on this road, and this road alone."

All this talk about faith troubled Jack. *How can I get anywhere in this journey? I don't have much faith right now.*

Azarel looked into his eyes and Jack suddenly found the courage to speak what was on his heart. "I have to be honest with you, Azarel. I am in the midst of a crisis of faith. God has seemed miles away from any of my prayers. I guess I'm not quite sure what I believe anymore. It seems like a great chasm has opened up in the 18 inches between my head and my heart. They never seem to meet."

"Yes, Jack, I understand those 18 inches very well. It has become an ugly plague upon you modern humans. You have acquired much knowledge because you have studied hard. Though you don't realize it, you have allowed yourself to become exceedingly proud. Jack, you have sought to know God out of your knowledge and out of your ability, not out of your brokenness and need, which you have yet to see.

"You have studied the Scriptures. Don't you know God only reveals Himself to those who come to Him as children? Don't you know you can only approach Him through His favor, not by your own efforts or abilities?

The Father resists the proud but gives grace to the humble."

Offended, Jack tensed his jaws.

"Azarel, how can you say this? I am not a proud man. If you don't believe me, ask anyone who knows me."

"Jack, I believe you really think that's true. No one can see their own pride; it must be revealed to them. Though you deny it, in your heart you still think you stand before God by your effort and by your ability to know Him. The only way He will break through that delusion is by insulting your mind and breaking your pride, thus exposing the futility of your reasoning and human effort. Jack, you have not yet been insulted by His message. Until you have, the Father King will continue to seem miles away, and the door to the heavens will continue to be closed."

Lips now pursed and face flushed, Jack raised his voice, "Azarel, you are mistaken. I am NOT proud! I have NEVER been proud! I have grown up in church my whole life and have ALWAYS known my need for God!"

Jack paused and took a deep breath. Quickly exhaling, he continued, "And what do you mean, the healing of my soul? My soul is just fine, thank you!"

Jack smugly thrust his chin into the air, only to suddenly double over in pain.

"Auggh! My side!" Jack gasped for air while quickly grasping his side.

Azarel began, "The pain you feel is the thorn you've been granted; and not you alone, but all who have ever lived on earth.

"The Thorn is the Prod of God, reminding man of his utter need for divine intervention to make him pure.

Adam's sinful stain ever permeates the blood of man—he can never truly clean himself. Though all are born with the Thorn, most have numbed themselves to its pain. I have not only come to reveal the Way *before* you, but the Way *within* you.

"The Thorn is one of the Father's gifts to bring you the healing purge your soul needs. If you allow yourself to feel its pain, it will drive you to your knees. The one who feels the pain has been broken by the Thorn, and his brokenness leads him to wholeness."

"But...the pain," replied Jack, "I don't understand... it's in my side, not my soul, it's..."

Suddenly a terrible sound began to echo off the trees, the rocks, and the very air surrounding them. This "sound" was a wail, and the wail was the most awful and painful sounding noise he had ever heard. Without even feeling the blood slowly dripping out from under his ribs, Jack stood with tears streaming down his face, frightened at the depth of agony he was hearing. In a kind of delayed reaction, Jack gripped his side. Feeling his wound, he doubled over in pain. Azarel stepped over, touched the wound, and as it instantly stopped bleeding, so too the awful wail ceased.

"What you have just heard, Jack, is the cry of your soul. It is the cry of frustrated efforts, the cry of loss, the cry of all your pain and sorrows. You have never noticed it because you have always denied it. It is the cry of every soul, but it can never really be heard until it is honestly reckoned as actually being real. It is the same as the wail of Adam and Eve when they suddenly realized that they had forever been thrust from the Garden, never to return again. It even brings tears to the Creator Himself. However, nothing can be changed until a person ceases to ignore reality."

In confusion, Jack covered his face with his hands and sobbed. "I just don't understand, Azarel, I am hopeless. Your words don't make sense to me." Dropping his hands, Jack pleaded, "What can I do?"

"Jack, you will continue to remain a pauper if you keep your eyes focused on yourself and wallow in your inability. This is why you are here, and this is why I was summoned. If you choose to go on this journey, my presence will always remain with you. At times, it will be veiled—sometimes by the Father King's choice and other times by your own neglect. However, neither the Father King nor I will force you to go on this journey, but if you choose to go, you will find what you have always sought but could never discover. You will find LIFE!"

"This is all so confusing..." After a few moments of silence, Jack soberly spoke, "I trust you. Yes, I will go."

With a large smile on his face, Azarel replied, "Then welcome to the Journey of Honest Reckoning, Mr. Jack Avery."

Chapter Three

THE MIRROR OF TRUTH

Its red bricks foot-beaten and weather-worn, the Pathway of Faith glistened in the sun as it wound its way into the dense forest. The huge arm-like limbs of the great hemlocks lining the edge of the trail bobbed and swayed in the wind, bidding welcome to the new traveler. As the trees rustled in the wind, the entire forest seemed to join in the welcome. It was as though Jack heard a thousand voices, majestic in chorus, within his heart. In reality he was "sensing" rather than hearing with his ears—a new experience for him. Calling, beckoning, the "wooded" choir sang forth:

Come! Come!
Come follow the Path.
Stay on the Way.
Lay hold of persistence.
Do not delay!"

Jack looked curiously at his guide.

Azarel smiled and explained, "You are learning how to hear in a new dimension, Jack."

"It is the most beautiful thing I ever heard!" Jack stood awestruck in the wake of heaven's music unveiled.

Azarel looked at Jack, raised his eyebrows and nodded at the path. Grinning, Jack said, "Let's go, Azarel!" and together they began down the path.

As the music faded into the distance, Azarel turned to Jack and pointed at his backpack. "Why are you carrying your provisions?"

Jack stopped and with much bewilderment looked at his companion. "What do you mean?"

"Whatever you will need shall be provided. All you have to do is believe."

"You mean that you want me to leave my backpack here and just trust the Father King for whatever I need?"

"Exactly."

"This is crazy," said Jack. "I have never done anything like this before."

"Well then, you have never trusted Him."

Jack winced and tried to muster up his courage. "I will choose to trust, but you must help me."

"That's my job."

"Then I'll do it."

Dropping his heavy pack, Jack straightened his shoulders, took a deep breath, and strode forward with a look of determination on his face. Thus they began their journey. After three hours of hiking, the travelers came to a fork in the road. In the middle stood a wooden sign planted in a bed of rhododendron bushes, small rocks, and mountain ferns. It read:

I desire truth in the inward parts, and in the hidden part, I will make you to know wisdom...
If you desire to see the real truth of your heart, go right... otherwise proceed to the left.

Jack looked at Azarel, then at the sign, and immediately turned to his right. The path meandered for a short way until just beyond one of the bends next to a clump of flowering azaleas stood a large, oval mirror about seven feet high and four feet wide. Around the mirror was a golden frame ornately designed with carvings of flowers, vines, and scrolls. Attached on each side was a bronze pillar anchoring it into the ground.

Bewildered, Jack looked at Azarel, "What is this?"

"You chose to see the truth—this is the Mirror of Truth. All who look into it see the true condition of their hearts as they come face to face with what is in them. No one will see the same thing. Your task is to gaze into this mirror and not turn away, no matter what you see. Are you willing to look?"

Cautiously, Jack stepped forward, looking only at the ground until he was standing in front of the huge mirror. "Yes, I'm willing."

As Jack slowly raised his head and fixed his eyes onto his reflected image, he gasped as he beheld what appeared to be four elf-like creatures attached to his body. One was standing on his head, one was swinging merrily from the back of his neck, one firmly held onto his shoulder, and one clutched his left leg.

"Who are these…uhh…or …what are these…?" Why are they on me? Get off!"

Jack began flailing his arms over every place on which the elves stood—only to smack his own body and beat the air.

"Why can't I get rid of them?" Jack turned to Azarel, hoping to find some answer to his predicament.

"They are a part of you, Jack. You can't fight them, knock them off, or hurt them with your *physical* self—only your actions and words will be able to do that. You'll see what I mean. But they can touch you, and you will feel them. They are intimately involved in the sensations of your physical body, as they have always been."

Jack turned back at the mirror to stare at these weird creatures, trying to understand what Azarel had just said. Finally he shook his head and asked, "What do I call them?"

Suddenly, in a jumbled hodgepodge of introductions, the creatures all began to speak at once.

"Wait, wait...one at a time!" Suddenly, in a flood of revelation, Jack recognized them as one who remembers old acquaintances but can't quite place who they are. Yes, though he had never actually seen them before, he had been aware of their presence for many years... aware at least at some level. Now that awareness had moved to his conscious level.

"You, on my head, what's your name?"

The creature stood on his large feet, which ruffled Jack's hair as his toes grasped it to help balance himself. "Well, Jack, we are your offspring. Our mother is Human Nature, and between you and her were we conceived. He affected quite a theatrical bow and announced, "Maskon is my name and performance is my game."

Jack looked at Azarel. "Is this true?"

"Yes, it is Jack. These creatures are the result of the way you have chosen to live and what you have come to believe. You asked to see what is in you, and here it is."

Jack looked back into the mirror and then spoke to the elf swinging around from the back of his neck, "Who are you?"

Swelling up with pride, this creature boomed forth, "I am Gnosis, or Professor Gnosis if you prefer. I've spent many an hour helping you to study so you will know all there is to know about God. If it weren't for me, you would never have been made youth pastor, you know." Gnosis sniffed a little at the thought.

"And you...?" pointing to his left shoulder, Jack asked, "What is your name?"

As this creature dug his fingers into Jack's shoulder, simultaneously Jack felt anxiety rushing through his own body.

"Uh, wel-l-l... m-m-my name... is-s-s...Phobion."

Not wanting to hear any more from this one, Jack looked down at the last creature gripping his knee, "And who are you?"

Hanging on for dear life with his little suction cupped hands secure as they could be, the creature quickly answered, "Oh, I'm Cleavon, please don't shake me off. I need to stay here. I won't be a burden to you, I promise!" Helplessness suddenly pricked Jack's heart. He gritted his teeth, and his heart began to beat just a little bit faster.

Looking up and down at his image in the mirror, Jack could hardly believe his eyes. His forehead began to throb until he finally looked over at Azarel. "Though I can't deny it, I still can hardly take all this in. No wonder I have felt so awful! Just look at what's on me!"

"Jack, for the first time in your life you are beginning to see undiluted truth. You are seeing *what really is*, not what you want to see. Such vision hurts, but it is necessary for all who desire the life that you crave. Mostly these characters will be invisible. At times, though, they will appear so that you can learn how to deal with them."

Jack stood still, deep in thought, trying to understand this new reality of himself... a monstrous reality. *If this is at the beginning of the path, what's coming down the road?*

Chapter Four

BREAD AND WATER

Like a knife, the Mirror of Truth began to slice away every bit of denial and self-righteousness Jack had covered himself with. For the first time, Jack glimpsed some of the depth of his guilt, and each elf was evidence of his indictment. Realizing that their presence was the direct result of choices he had made and attitudes he had held throughout his years, Jack felt mixed emotions surging through him—he felt sick, angry, offended, and trapped in turn.

Eventually Jack realized the creatures had disappeared, though he was still fully aware of their presence. Finding a rock, he sank down, feeling weak and short of breath.

After a few minutes, he looked up at Azarel. "How can I ever be healthy with these vexing creatures all over me?"

With compassion in his eyes, Azarel walked over and pointed his finger at Jack's heart. "Yes, vexing is what they are, but control is not something they possess.

These characters are simply the result of choices you've made, and they will continue to exist based on the choices you will continue to make and the ones you will avoid making. You have the power to choose—it has not been so granted to them. As you choose rightly in faith and courage, though they may rage at you, they cannot control you."

"But Azarel, how do I choose rightly? I'm not sure that I have the faith or courage to do it."

Azarel pointed to the path on which they stood, "See this, Jack? This is the path you must follow—you will know it for its narrowness and blood-red color. Heaven's blood marks the path—without the blood there is no path. The cost of this path was the piercing of the Father King's heart—a cost no less than the life of His one Son, a perfect sacrifice. The death of the Son completed the Pathway of Faith and made the Father King's authority accessible to all who walk upon it. The Father King raised His Son back to life and now He lives to help all the children of the Father King defeat their enemies and find the destiny marked for each of their lives. The blood lays claim to all who choose to journey its way. No power in heaven or earth can deter the feet that walk on this crimson path, except one—the power of choice.

"To choose rightly, Jack, you must ruthlessly remain on this Pathway of Faith. As long as you walk this way, you will come to know a power not your own. Your challenge will be to refrain from the alluring Trails of Intellect and Emotion. They wind around in circles and spirals of all sorts until you end up thoroughly lost. If you watch carefully for them, you can quickly recognize the difference—their color is never red. Don't worry so much about faith and courage, Jack. These virtues are not so much qualities one develops and owns as they are fragrances released from the choices one makes. One is kept on the pathway not by some unusual faith, but by everyday faithfulness; and one is driven on not by courage, but by daily obedience. Faith and courage are the supernatural fragrances emanating from the life that is faithful and obedient to the Father King."

"I feel so overwhelmed by all this. Azarel, I'll never make it without your help."

"That's why I am here." Azarel smiled fondly at him. "For the first time in your life, you are recognizing your insufficiency."

"Another thing—you said we are on the Journey of Honest Reckoning and going to the place of wholeness and healing of my soul. How will I know when we have arrived?"

"You will know, Jack. It will be most unmistakable. Our destination leads to the realm of the One who sent me and to the territory of His kingdom. There you will meet the Builder of this path and the Perfector of your faith."

"I can hardly wait! Such a place must be truly amazing!"

"Yes, it is amazing, but so too is the sacrifice and cost required to appreciate the life of that place. In that life, death is not to be feared. All the inhabitants, though still mortal, have embraced death's sting by the daily sacrifice of humble submission to the Father King."

"Azarel, this is too much for me to take in right now. My head is spinning. It sounds wonderful and yet frightening at the same time."

Nodding in agreement, Azarel explained, "So it is, and so it remains even like a dream. At this point in your journey, the gaps of your understanding are filled in with the colors of fantasy, for that is all one can do, and so your understanding remains more like a dream than reality. Your understanding will be increased the farther we journey, for the ways of the Kingdom must first be experienced before the knowledge of such a life can be grasped. And so, what seems fantasy and dream-like now will eventually seem as normal as that which you currently call 'reality.'"

Sitting down on a nearby rock, Azarel began to share with Jack, "I will plainly tell you about the Kingdom. Though you won't understand much of it, you still must hear it now. Later it will make more sense to you. I won't speak again of these things until the end of your journey when you finally see the Kingdom.

"Destiny and purpose are given to all the citizens of this kingdom, for they themselves have become co-partners in all the regal plans and omniscient decrees of the Father King Himself. All citizens, though originally subjects and slaves, are declared heirs and children of this King. All who submit their rights and claims to Him are accordingly given the scepter of His rule, which releases His authority in their lives. Though access to His authority is always available for each citizen, not all will lay hold of it. In this kingdom, there exist two doorways through which such authority is accessed. Only those citizens who learn how to enter these doorways are those who can lay hold of the King's authority.

"First, there is an internal doorway in the heart of each citizen. On the other side of this door is found the throne of the Father King. Though it is a mystery, somehow it is true that, through the spirit of each citizen, access to the authority of the Father King is gained. Only those who have the right key are able to access His authority that lies within, ready to be used. In the realm of this kingdom, faith alone is the key that unlocks this door. In the heart of each citizen is given a measure of faith, but to lay hold of this key is a difficult challenge. To lay hold of this key one must learn to trust the King's words more than anything else—more than circumstances, more than one's intellect, and more than one's talents or abilities.

"Living by such faith is the greatest challenge in the realm of the Father King because His enemies are constantly challenging such trust among the citizenry. Nevertheless, as various citizens learn how to lay hold of their faith, then their spirit's doorway opens and they lay hold of this power through the words of their mouths and the works of their hands so that the Kingdom is established, extended, and gloriously displayed.

"The second doorway you will learn more about later. However, it is sufficient to say that it can be obscure and many times is hidden—but when the citizen crawls through it, perfect authority for the task at hand is instantly released."

Pausing in his words, Azarel reflected, "That which I've shared is now only partially understood, but know this much—you have gained a key of understanding. Use it wisely to unlock the value of significance for the struggles you will face. Otherwise hopelessness may derail you from completing your journey."

Azarel paused a few moments in silence to let his words sink into Jack's mind. Standing up, he declared, "Enough of this for now. Too much talking is empty until the Kingdom ways have been learned. We still have a long way to go."

Jack was still feeling less than enthusiastic—he didn't like the idea of following a trail without knowing what was ahead. However, he held onto Azarel's words that he would understand more later and forced himself to stand.

Suddenly, all the creatures appeared on Jack and started to complain. Each one loudly voiced their objections to proceeding on the journey, but Maskon was the most cantankerous of them all.

Maskon blurted out, "How are we going to get there? How long is it going to take? I need a map or a script to follow so that we can have a successful outcome to our efforts. After all, my reputation as a successful traveler is at stake, and I have only so much time to allow for this trip!"

Azarel calmly responded, "There is no map except the Pathway of Faith. You must simply trust it."

"That's easy for you to say. You've been there before!"

On and on Maskon complained as Jack and Azarel hiked. Finally Jack got so weary of the complaining that he said to Azarel, "I wish Maskon would be quiet. He's starting to discourage me."

"Then tell him to stop."

"You think he'll listen?"

"He *must* do what you say, Jack. You have the power of choice, remember?"

"Okay, then." Jack turned to Maskon and, in a very calm voice began, "Maskon, you need to be quiet. You need to stop complaining right now. We told you that we aren't stopping and…"

"I'm sorry," interrupted Maskon, "but I'm concerned that we don't have a schedule... I really don't think we should go any further without a schedule or map. What lies ahead? We don't even know what we are going to run into. And what about..."

With that, Jack finally snapped. "Stop it! Be quiet! You are not in charge! We are all learning to trust and walk by faith and YOU MUST COOPERATE!"

Maskon instantly clammed up and not another peep was heard out of him for quite some time.

Relieved, Jack turned to Azarel. "I'm hungry. What are we going to eat? We left the pack at the entrance, and it had all the food."

"Jack, Jack, your faith is so small. Besides, the pack could not hold food for the entire journey—it would have eventually run out. Remember, on the Journey of Honest Reckoning you will come to know the Father King as Provider. He knows what you have need of even before you can realize your need. He has made provision even before provision is needed. You could not have learned true faith without discarding your backpack. On this journey, you will learn that no man is his own provider. We are all helpless without our Father to care for us. You'll learn that we are all simply beggars before the loving hand of God. Nothing can change this fact. We can fight it and we can deny it, but nothing can change it."

Jack hung his head. "I guess you're right. I feel so clumsy in this school of faith. I've studied about it but never really experienced it."

"Old mindsets, Jack, are hard to change. To study about something is one thing, but to learn a new way to live is quite another. Faith is not something inherent in you. It derives its power from the Source—the Provider. Once you have met the Provider you will become acquainted with faith—it issues from His very presence and gets lodged in your heart."

As they walked on together, Azarel continued to expound on the meaning of true faith and courage. The longer they talked, the clearer things became for Jack, as though a fog was beginning to lift from his mind. Jack's new openness and humility became the fertile soil for the seeds of life Azarel was sowing into his soul.

Recognizing the need for a lesson from personal experience, Azarel stopped walking and looked at Jack, "Will you believe with me?"

"Yes," Jack said quickly, "but for what?"

"Close your eyes and pray with me." Azarel looked up to heaven and with child-like confidence called out, "Father, Provider... Give us this day our daily bread! Amen."

Jack added his own "Amen" just in time to open his eyes and see outstretched before them a table on which an abundance of rolls and a pitcher of ice cold water had been placed. With the Rolls of Provision and Water of Life, they had more than enough for their needs. They sat down on comfortable chairs set on each side of the table and began to eat. Breezes of pure peace gently blew through the trees. Jack rested his hands on the table and soaked in the glorious wind. After a few minutes, they heard a voice speak:

I am Your Provider.
I love you and I will care for you.
Humbly receive and boldly believe...
And you will know My salvation.

Gently the voice trailed off, leaving Jack awestruck

with the reality that the Father King had just addressed him.

Jack tried to make sense of what he had just experienced. Unmistakably, the voice itself was in the wind, but it was not the wind. It was so mysterious that for a brief moment Jack was tempted to doubt it had even happened. He began to wonder if there had really even been a voice, or if perhaps he had simply mistaken the sound of the wind.

Azarel, seeing Jack's bewilderment, explained, "You hear the wind with your ears and feel it with your body, for it is the breath of God. It is in your heart where you have heard His voice—your heart has its own ears and eyes. To see and hear more rightly with one's heart is the aim of this journey, Jack. But never forget that just outside the doorway of your heart creeps Discrediting Doubt, seeking to refute any act of faith experienced within that doorway by using simple explanations of rational proof. The battle is won initially by choice but eventually choice will be strengthened by experience. This you shall see as the miles on our narrow path move from before us to behind us."

Together, teacher and student continued feasting like kings, eating to their hearts' content. Just as they finished, Jack reached into the bowl of rolls and thrust six of them into his coat pocket. Azarel turned to Jack and warned, "Eat only what you need. The rest will be provided. Remember our prayer—'Give us this day our daily bread.'"

"Okay." Yet, even as the words left his mouth, a sudden twinge of doubt grabbed his heart and, as though almost unable to help himself, he pulled out only five of the six, leaving one remaining roll in his pocket. After putting the five others back into the bowl, he joined Azarel on the pathway.

No one will ever know... I'm just playing it safe, Jack reassured himself. But a seed of doubt was now planted in his soul, the effect of which would soon be revealed and its power released.

And the echo continued, *I'm just playing it safe... just being sure.*

Chapter Five

THE CLOUDS OF DESPAIR

Two hours of hiking passed when Jack's thoughts returned to his life back home, which now seemed as far away as another galaxy. As his mind began to focus on unanswered questions in his life, Jack's head began to throb. *Why have I been so tired lately? Why have I felt so anxious about my life when everything seems to be going so great? Am I really in the right job or should I return to being a youth pastor? Is Julie the right woman for me? How can I ever know the answers? Where is God when I need Him? Sometimes He seems so far away. Will I ever make anything of my life?*

These thoughts played over and over in his mind like one of those tunes you can't get out of your head. Jack was so caught up in his own thoughts that he hadn't realized that Azarel was nowhere to be seen.

Phobion popped up on Jack's shoulder and whispered in his ear, "This hike is not going to get you anywhere… you should turn back now while you have the chance. You don't know what might be lurking around the next corner."

Professor Gnosis, with a determined air, now was standing on Jack's head impatiently tapping his foot. With his arms folded, he sternly looked down and bombarded Jack: "What's next? You know you don't have a plan for your life. And you are much too smart to think that a simple hike is what you need to fix everything. Let's go back, Jack, and we'll study this out logically."

Jack's heart began to race when Cleavon suddenly appeared down below on Jack's left leg. He suctioned-cupped himself up to Jack's ear and whispered, "Jack, you need to get married; you need the companionship. You can't afford to lose Julie. Why not turn back and see if she wants to elope with you. That way you can be sure you won't lose her. Don't wait. You never know if she'll get mad because you're off by yourself for the weekend. She might even call up her old boy friend while you're gone…"

Jack shook his head violently as if to try and clear his mind and knock the characters to the ground. When they saw his actions, they knew Jack was afraid, vulnerable, and desperately insecure. With their mission accomplished for the time being, they quietly faded away.

Jack didn't notice that the sky had become cloudy and dark because he was so distracted with his thoughts. As the darkness increased, he became so fixated on the anxious thoughts swirling through his head that he ceased to pay attention to where he was hiking. He unwittingly drifted off the Pathway of Faith and began trekking down a wider side trail. He never saw the sign indicating he was heading toward the Bog of Obsessive Introspection. He just continued down the trail, thinking about all of the unresolved issues of his life, trying to come up with answers for his situation back home. Jack kept probing his emotions, trying to determine how he really felt, as though he could find the answers in his feelings. But no answers were forthcoming and so he felt even more confused than before. His eyes now were only on himself and not on where he was going.

Rain began to fall, first as a mist then as a pounding downpour. The ground was so soggy that it was quickly becoming a perilous trap. He began to feel the poking and prodding of the Thorn, but only faintly because he was so focused on his thoughts. Off in the distance, the voice of Azarel could be heard, calling out to Jack.

Jack was quickly losing his ability to navigate, although he wasn't even aware of it. Each step became increasingly difficult. Eventually he could barely even take one step either forward or backward. His thoughts now perfectly paralleled his situation—he was stuck in them without a way out. Jack had become so overwhelmed with the questions of his past and reconciling the issues of his present that, just as he decided he wanted to move forward with his present job, he paused, wondering if that was really best. When he finally decided that he should go ahead, Professor Gnosis would pop up and remind him of all his studies that he had labored over to reach the position of youth pastor. "Surely you want to make Senior Pastor one day, Jack," Gnosis challenged him. Jack then paused to consider that perhaps it was better for him to go back to his old position as youth pastor. Somehow in this awful place every step Jack took came to symbolize an unresolved issue or concern needing to be figured out.

Phobion dug deeper in his shoulder saying, "You'll

have a wife soon. Stay with your job—you're making good money there. Don't rock the boat, Jack!"

Maskon grabbed the front of Jack's shirt and pleaded, "For heaven's sakes, man, your performance at the sales job is admirable. Everyone sees how well you're doing. Just work a little harder and you'll be top salesman!"

Eventually, Jack decided not to go anywhere until he could figure out what he was going to do with his life, and so he sank deeper into the mire.

Meanwhile, Azarel continued calling out to Jack to climb out of the bog and rejoin him on the Pathway of Faith, but Jack was so preoccupied that he still didn't hear. The mud and muck that he sank into was only a foot deep in the beginning but had become twice as deep in the last several minutes. Jack's body became increasingly bent over trying to maneuver in it. The coldness and pressure of the mud, now above his knees, was still not registering in Jack's awareness.

Suddenly, like a bolt of lightning, Jack felt a fiery piercing in his side. Jack was now thrust out of his preoccupied thinking as he grasped his side. He suddenly became aware of his peril, and panicked as desperation crashed over him.

"Azarel, Azarel! Where are you?"

Jack was frantically trying to lift his legs out of the muck, only to topple down into it, and when he managed to stand back up, the mire was even deeper.

"Azarel! Azarel!"

Breathing heavier and heavier, Jack was looking everywhere and listening above the pounding rain for even the faintest sound of his companion.

Finally he heard Azarel calling faintly, but what was it? What was this Jack was hearing? A song? In the midst of Jack's panic, Azarel was singing!

"Don't pay any attention to him, Jack. He can't care much about you if all he does is sing when you're calling for help!" Phobion said.

"There must be something you studied in one of your classes that will help you here," Gnosis added. "Think, Jack, there must be a logical way out of this!"

The four characters were all huddled above Jack's waist, not liking the situation they were in at all. "This doesn't look good, Jack." Maskon said. "Do something for goodness sake. What will people think if you drown in all this mess?"

"Quiet, all of you. I can't hear Azarel above all your nonsense!" They clamped their mouths shut and once again faded away.

The mud reached all the way up to Jack's neck when the rain finally let up. At last Jack could hear Azarel singing a song of deliverance over him. The more Jack listened, the more it enveloped him. Bursting and exploding within the air around him, the song now powerfully permeated everything. Seven times it was sung, each time louder than the last with greater bursts of energy.

Gaze upward, gaze high;
Creator is beckoning,
Look up to the sky!
Posture, unbend.
Stand straight, stand tall,
Be rooted in Him!

Reach out in His name
And salvation you'll see.
Confess and proclaim,
Lay hold of your key!

On the seventh time, just as Jack heard the last phrase, "Reach out!" with all his strength, he shoved his hands up out of the muck, straightened out his body as best he could, and reached upward to heaven. He screamed, "Father! Creator! Help me!"

Immediately an invisible rope, feeling as light as the wind, wrapped itself around Jack's wrists and gently pulled him up and out of the bog and deposited him on higher ground. Immediately loud thunder exploded and released a new deluge of rain, which completely drenched Jack, washing off every bit of mud from his body and clothes. Then the wind-rope that was around his wrists suddenly exploded into a swirling mass which completely dried him off. Next it formed the funnel shape of a tornado, rising higher and higher until it attacked the clouds, ripping them apart and dispersing them in every possible direction until they were nowhere to be seen. Finally it disappeared into the sky, and there was brightness and light shining from the sun.

Everything became quiet and still. Jack stood up, staring down at the bog from which he was delivered. All he could hear was his breathing.

A smile spread over Jack's face. He took a deep breath, turned and yelled, "Azarel!" sprinting all the way back to the Pathway of Faith as his heart burst with joy and gratefulness at his deliverance.

Finally, back on the right path, Jack was overwhelmed by the sudden revelation that life was no longer about having all the right answers as much as simply being in the Father King's presence.

Jack could still feel the soreness of the wound in his side. He affectionately put his hand over it and with tears in his eyes, whispered toward heaven, "Oh thank

You, precious Father King. Thank you for my Thorn—You are teaching me to know my need of You."

Azarel greeted him warmly, and Jack looked into his friend's eyes. Somehow he could feel the smile of God, high in the sky, penetrating down through every wave of the dancing light around them. In a gentle rustling of the wind, Jack faintly heard the words, "Well done. Well done." Jack knew the Father King was watching them. Then all was still and quiet once again.

"Jack, you will face those ugly clouds of despair again and again, but on this journey you will learn how to fight and prevail over them." Azarel paused, then asked, "Do you feel a sensation in your chest right now?"

"Yes. I feel peace, incredible peace, I feel the presence of the Father King. My questions and problems seem so small and insignificant right now, as if I've been asking all the wrong questions."

"This peace you feel is fullness of life that you and all men seek after. The horrible delusion is to think that such life is found in answers, people, and things. You must fight to maintain this peace, this centered focus."

"What do you mean I must fight?"

"Jack, the power of those clouds is in the respect and authority you give to your natural thinking—thinking unchecked with the words of truth spoken by the Father King. When you strayed off the Pathway of Faith and onto the Trail of Intellect, you almost experienced your own demise. The bog you just encountered was not ordained by the Father King. You must fight to keep yourself away from such places. But there shall be other clouds, storms, and muddy paths you must journey through, ones which the Creator has allowed for your growth. For such trials though, He always releases the necessary grace for your victory.

"The purpose of your Thorn, Jack, is to expose your need to completely trust the Father King for everything. This journey of life is also a journey of death, the death of all that is unholy within you. You must come to love such a death more than life itself, for therein is found true life—resurrection life.

"Much of this journey has to do with rightly knowing the truth. The peril you faced was the result of allowing the needs of your life to drive you deeper and deeper into yourself with the false hope that you could save yourself.

"Jack, we have talked much about the power of choice. Your enemy just tried to paralyze you from making any choice and thereby strip you of this power. As long as you do not decisively resist his lies, you will ultimately be led in the direction he intends. In such desperate situations, there is no such thing as staying on neutral ground. You either advance or lose ground.

"It was your Thorn, the Prod of God, that saved you. Because of it, you turned your face upward toward the Father. Like a burning cattle's prod, the Thorn is teaching you how to rightly think, walk, and live."

Azarel noticed that Jack looked very puzzled. "You'll see what I mean, Jack Avery... you will soon see indeed. Now let's move on, we still have a good way to go until the mountain."

"The mountain?" asked Jack. "What mountain?"

"We're going to the Mountain of Vision, where you will see visions of truth to help you better understand all we've been talking about."

Chapter Six

MASKS OF DECEPTION

As Jack walked down the pathway with Azarel, his mind pondered all the things he had experienced. After a few hours of hiking, he grew weary and began looking for a place to rest. Finding a large rock, they both gratefully sat down.

On the nearest side of the Pathway of Faith, Jack noticed a cluster of what appeared to be poles or rods, each about four feet high, that were stuck into the ground. Connected to the top of each pole was a mask, looking oddly out of place in the forest.

"What are these?" asked Jack.

Out popped Maskon in a delightful mood. "These, my dear Jack, are tools of my trade! With them I can go anywhere and be anyone I like. My, my, they are wonderful creations! I haven't seen such workmanship in a long time."

"I didn't ask you!" Jack grumbled.

"These are Masks of Deception," Azarel began. "By them mankind denies the pain of honest truth in exchange for the comfort of denial and ignorance. Watch and see what happens when someone encounters them. By the way, never look squarely into them—they will surely make you act contrary to the truth."

Azarel pointed at a trail with a large sign labeled "Deceit" that came down from a heavily wooded hill, crossed over the Pathway of Faith, and continued on the other side.

Soon they heard a sound of lighthearted whistling coming closer and closer until they saw a man skip out of the woods. He stopped on the Pathway of Faith and stared at Jack.

"Ah... hello... who are you?" Jack asked.

"Who am I? Everybody knows me...except you, I guess. Ha! Ha! Nevertheless, I will tell you. My name is Everyman."

"Well, Everyman, I am pleased to make your acquaintance. My name is Jack Avery. Please tell me, I am curious to know, where are you are so happily going today?"

"I am seeking life, seeking to find the ultimate one thing all people seek."

"Wait!" exclaimed Jack. "I'm on the same journey too!"

"Really? What is your destination? I notice that your path is different than mine."

"I'm going to the Kingdom of the Father King. I still have a long way to go, but I'm being prepared along the way so that I may become one of its citizens."

"Why are you going *there*, Jack? Do you really believe that fairy tale about the Father King and His Kingdom? Come with me—I'll show you the city of your dreams. Follow me to the City of Imageon where I am told the desires of my heart and the thoughts of my mind will find their fullest expression."

"Sounds delightful!" Maskon (who had been listening closely) interrupted. "I think we should set off right away with this engaging gentleman. After all, he looks like he knows exactly where he's going!"

Just as Jack was about to speak sharply to Maskon, he suddenly noticed a gaping, bloody, oozing wound from the side of Everyman. "You're injured! What happened to you?"

The wound smelled of putrid rotting flesh. It was dripping with a greenish yellow fluid, mixed with watery blood.

Everyman looked confused. He looked at his side, touching and squeezing the area where the wound was, making more fluid spill out.

"You're crazy! What are you talking about? I don't have any wound."

Even Maskon at first looked askance before he regained his composure. "Sure, Jack, it's nothing to worry about."

Jack stood awkwardly, still staring at Everyman's side. "Ahh... h-h-how did you learn of this city where you're going?"

"Divine visitation. I met a luminous angel. He said I would find perfect happiness if I made it to this city. There I will become like a god because I will have no more needs. He said all I have to do is follow these broad winding trails to my heart's content—and they would lead me to the doors of the city. And you—where did you hear of your fairy tale?"

"Oh," said Jack, "it's not a fairy tale, I'm sure of that. But I heard it from my friend here. His name is Azarel. Everyman, meet Azarel."

"Real funny Jack, I don't see anybody. You're a real joker," laughed Everyman. "You should come with me, we'd have a lot of fun, I can tell."

Jack looked at Azarel in confusion.

"Jack, Everyman can't see or hear me because he has given himself over to deception. Neither does he see or feel the wound of his Thorn, thus he is unaware of the rotting within him. He cannot know the truth of which I speak until he confesses his error and begins to seek what he has consciously denied. He knows the truth, but until he confesses his error he'll forever be lost. Watch and see what I mean."

Just then, exploding from the midst of the atmosphere around them, and out over the hills and through the trees came the horrible Cry of the Thorn once again. Jack looked over at Everyman to see him with an ashen face and then a tear trickling down his cheek.

Then, just as quickly, Everyman, as though waking out of a daydream, shook his head, brushed the tear away, and slapped his face saying, "I didn't hear anything. No sirree, nothing at all."

Jack looked at Everyman in utter amazement, "Yes, you did! And you still do! It's echoing all around us!"

Although Everyman's brow was wet with sweat now, he stubbornly replied, "N-N-N-No way." Conveniently changing the subject, Everyman walked over to the poles and asked, "Hey, what's on this pole over here? That one looks like a soldier!"

"No!" cried Jack, "Don't look into it! Don't..."

Suddenly the mask came flying off the pole and completely attached itself to the face of Everyman. It knocked him over into a puddle of mud and sent him kicking and screaming on his back with his feet flailing in the air.

"Get this thing off me! Get it off now!" he yelled.

The scene was almost humorous because the mask didn't even fit him. Yet when Everyman got to his feet and looked down at the water, he caught the reflection of the mask covering his face and suddenly was content.

"Why, it fits just perfectly, and it's not really a mask, it's just an accurate representation of who I really am. I've always been a take charge kind of guy."

With newness of energy, Everyman sprung up from his spot and began marching as he crossed over the Pathway of Faith to continue along the same trail he had originally been following. As he headed down the hill, wearing his Mask of Deception, he yelled back, "You'll see Jack, you'll see that I'm right and you are wrong! Go ahead follow your little myth! Go ahead and see where it leads you!"

Maskon stared after him and began to shake Jack's head. "Go after him, Jack. I think he's really got something there. Look how that soldier's face has changed him—he's really going somewhere now. He'd impress everyone I know!"

Jack frowned down at the little creature so hard he faded right away.

Azarel turned to Jack, shaking his head sadly. "Someday he will have to face the truth, for it is appointed on the final day that all men will face the truth. Everyman is afraid to face the truth honestly, for he is afraid of what might be exposed. He prefers his darkness to the light of truth, so he lives a lie and pretends to be better than he knows he is. I don't think you realized it, but the happy face he had been wearing when we first saw him was just another mask. Jack, to face oneself is one of the greatest challenges a mortal will ever face.

True strength only comes after the glorious revelation of one's miserable weakness, but rarely does such revelation ever penetrate the power of a mask. Enough talk! Let us go on."

After walking a short way Jack exclaimed, "Pheew! What's that smell? Auaghh! It's in my coat pocket!"

Jack put his hand into his pocket and, with a look of painful disgust, slowly pulled out a slimy mess.

"Gross! What is this black slime?"

Almost gagging from the nauseating smell, Jack turned his pocket inside out and began to knock the putrid mess off it. As it hit the ground, worms began to squirm out of it and slowly slither away. Jack looked to Azarel for an explanation as he wiped his filthy hand on his pants.

"Jack, on the Pathway of Faith you must learn to trust. I told you that the Provider would care for all your needs, but you did not trust me. Evidently you sought to secure your own well-being by slipping one of the rolls into your jacket. And now what was once a Roll of Provision by your Provider has become a rotting Roll of Unbelief from your enemy.

"You will learn more of this enemy, but know this much—he not only exists outside of you, roaming the reaches of the earth, but also within you. He sees any door or trail of unbelief found within you. Such things give him the right to travel your interior territory and wreck havoc in your soul.

"Hasn't our Provider been more than faithful? Why did you hide the bread? You have followed fear and not faith. The result you see is the decay of what once was good."

Jack fell to his knees, feeling the weight of his sin.

The pain in his side began to throb. For an instant he began to feel those familiar pangs of depression and self-condemnation.

Azarel, looking down at Jack, commanded, "Jack, embrace your Thorn—don't ignore it. Admit your weakness and receive the Father's strength!"

As Jack inwardly began to turn away from condemning himself, something deep within him began to rise up. Thorn's throb began to subside and Jack began to weep. He cried out to heaven, "Oh, Father, I am sorry. Forgive me for my sin of unbelief and faithlessness. Help me to be more faithful! You alone are my help and my hope!"

Touching his shoulder, Azarel declared, "Jack, your sin is forgiven; your heart is right. Receive mercy, receive grace. Your heart is honest and humble, and of such does God love to forgive. Stand up! Your sin is forgiven!"

When Jack stood up, the last bit of throbbing in his side completely ceased. Mercy and grace overwhelmed him—he could literally feel the old arguments of condemnation that used to plague him now slip away like the shedding of an old jacket.

He felt a sudden release of a deep cold pressure in his heart, and with it, the sensation of something like a root system being pulled out. In its place, a flood of faith came rushing in. Jack couldn't contain his joy any longer and burst forth into a spontaneous song of worship and praise. Never before had he known worship to be so sweet—never before had he felt such love and forgiveness.

As they continued down the path, Jack thought of his Thorn and realized that he had now begun to think of it as he might a special friend. He thought back to the roses he had recently seen at the florist's shop. *Maybe God has a purpose for the thorn after all.*

Chapter Seven

THE FOREST OF STILLNESS

As the encroaching evening dusk settled over Jack, he began to feel the fatigue of a long day. *I can't go any farther. I think my legs are going to collapse.*

Azarel stopped. "Jack, it's time to rest for the night."

"Where? We've seen nothing but forest."

"There," said Azarel pointing into the woods. Ahead and off to their right was a small log cabin tucked away back in the woods, with a stone walkway leading up to it. When Jack saw the friendly looking porch and the nearby bubbling brook, he felt wistfully nostalgic, as peaceful memories from his boyhood years flooded his mind. He had often had pleasant visits with his grandparents at their mountain cabin.

Jack was struck with an overwhelming awareness of the Father King's provision. In amazement he reflected, *How much energy and time I have wasted by worrying!*

When he opened the door, he could immediately see

that everything they needed was indeed already provided. On the kitchen table was a fully prepared meal of steak and potatoes, steaming hot and inviting. A blazing fire in the stone hearth quickly took away the descending evening chill. The travelers gratefully sat down at a darkly stained rustic table to a perfectly satisfying meal. As they ate and talked, recalling the exciting events of the day, Jack's spirit, too, felt renewed and refreshed. After dinner, he retired to one of the comfortable bedrooms and quickly fell into a peaceful sleep while Azarel sat lingering in a rocking chair, gazing into the fire.

The next morning a deliciously inviting smell of bacon and eggs wafted its way to Jack's nostrils. In the kitchen, he found breakfast once again already prepared and Azarel stretching his arms in the rocking chair.

"Did you do this, Azarel?"

"No, it wasn't me. I've been in this chair all night—I must have dozed off."

"Then who's making all these meals for us?"

"Oh, I guess you could say that the Father King has His ways of providing for His children."

"I'll say He does! This is great!"

"It is the Father's responsibility to provide your food, but it is your responsibility to eat it," explained Azarel.

"I would never complain about eating food like this!"

"All meals are not so appetizing, but they are all necessary," Azarel said. Jack was to remember this caution later, but now they both eagerly sat down at the table and quickly devoured their breakfast. After Jack put their dishes in the sink, Azarel stood at the door.

"Come, it is time to go."

They walked down the stone walkway to the

Pathway of Faith. Thoroughly refreshed, the travelers once again set off on their journey.

"How long until we reach the mountain?"

"It's still a fair distance away. First though, you need to complete another section of the journey."

"What's that?"

"You are about to begin the dangerous journey through the Forest of Stillness. You will come face to face with the two ravaging monsters who are mankind's greatest enemies, but all those who seek to reach the Mountain of Vision must pass through this forest. Look! There's the opening!"

As they approached the entrance, Azarel walked over to a nearby tree, picked up a shield that was leaning against it, and handed it to Jack.

"Here, take this. It is called the Shield of Faith. You will need it to defend yourself against the arrows that will be aimed at you."

"Arrows? What are you talking about, Azarel?"

"You will see. There is one more thing you need to know—you will not see nor hear me in this forest. Though you may feel alone, know that you are not. I will be with you, never doubt it."

As soon as Azarel disappeared, Phobion popped onto Jack's arm. "Jack, you don't have to go that way. Monsters don't sound good to me. Please Jack, don't go that way!"

Ignoring the creature hanging on his arm, Jack stomped into the forest, and immediately Phobion jumped over to his back and hid his face in Jack's shirt. Soon Jack felt the throbbing of his Thorn. All that remained were Azarel's last words, "Never doubt. Never doubt," reverberating in his mind.

Despite considerable pleas from Phobion for Jack to stop, he continued down the path that took him deeper and deeper into the heart of the woods. Eventually the forest became so dense with pine and hemlock trees that the sunlight could barely penetrate the thickness of the branches. It grew darker and quieter. The stillness was deafening, and it wasn't peacefully quiet, it was hauntingly quiet.

Phobion kept shaking uncontrollably so that Jack began to feel anxious. He eventually discovered that he could at least find some relief as long as he walked fast and kept his mind on anything other than the unnerving stillness. All Jack wanted was to get out of the forest and meet up with Azarel again. Why he was so unnerved by the forest, he couldn't understand.

The Pathway of Faith covered much hilly terrain—sometimes flat—but mostly up and down with increasingly bigger hills. Inevitably, Jack grew weary, and the pressing thought of his need to stop and rest filled him with dread. Finally, after several hours of hiking, Jack's body was completely exhausted and his heart was racing. "Azarel! Where are you? I need you now!"

He remembered Azarel's words: "Have faith, Jack. Have faith. All that you need shall be provided."

Jack closed his eyes and whispered a prayer: "I will believe, but I need to rest. Please take away this anxiety. Show me Your truth about this dread I feel."

When he opened his eyes, directly before him was a stately, brown leather wing-back chair in the middle of the Pathway of Faith, and beside it a sign which read: "The Chair of Rest and Truth." Attached at the bottom of each arm and draped up and over it was a golden rope about four feet long. Beautifully embroidered on the cords, in a type of medieval calligraphy, were the words:

"Cords of Love."

Odd, this is just what I asked for...rest and truth. He leaned the Shield of Faith against the chair and sat down.

Peace. Rest. Waves of refreshment pulsated over and through Jack—covering, penetrating, and massaging his weary legs and aching feet. Losing all sense of time, Jack consciously submerged himself into this amazing river as he sat totally intoxicated by the peace and rest of the chair.

Just as Jack convinced himself that it was time to get up and continue the torturous hike, a delightful breeze of pure peace blew over him. He leaned back to enjoy one final blessing and closed his eyes to take in its full effect.

In the same way that Jack "heard" the voice of the Father when Azarel had previously prayed for their food, so too, in the same way, did Jack now hear the voice of Azarel. Woven within the wind, Jack heard Azarel's question.

"Jack, do you trust Him? Do you trust the Father King?"

Surprised by such words, Jack opened his eyes, looked up, and exclaimed, "Yes! Oh Azarel, yes! I trust Him with all my heart!"

The wind stopped blowing, and everything became silent and still again. A mist of anxiety slowly descended, carrying with it a sense of ominous foreboding.

I-I-I-I g-g-guess I'd better get going. A cold shiver rolled down his back, while Phobion began to crawl down his arm.

Jack started to rise, but the cords suddenly became alive, causing Phobion to disappear in fright! They wrapped around Jack's chest, slammed him back into his seat, and then wrapped around the back side of the chair. Instantly the rope hardened like a rock, leaving Jack no chance of escape. Perplexed and afraid, Jack looked down at the cords.

Still they read: "Cords of Love."

Above him, Jack noticed ugly, black clouds blowing in. Then a barrage of thoughts came...

I shouldn't have rested so long. I'll never get out of this forest. I'm stuck here. I don't deserve to get out.

Thoughts continued to assault him in machine gun, rapid fire action until Jack felt like a complete failure.

It grew still darker.

Then on the screen of Jack's mind flashed the words: *Open your eyes and take up faith!*

Everything suddenly blurred. Jack blinked his eyes and out fell what looked something like wet fish scales. He blinked once again and couldn't believe the dreadful sight nearby. To his right was a terrifying dragon, far more hideous than he had imagined when Azarel first spoke of it. It measured about 60 feet from head to tail, with half of the length found in the tail. It was fully covered with an armor of red glistening scales trailing from its head to its feet. Its torso was a combination of man and serpent, ending in amphibious-like arms in the upper extremity, and legs in the lower regions resembling those of a mammoth-sized lizard. Each of its long feet ended with six black dagger-like nails that clasped the large, fallen oak tree on which it perched.

Its face was almost rectangular with piercing red eyes and an evil grimace that revealed its large, sharp teeth. Foul smelling saliva dripped from its protruding nose and elongated mouth. Down the back of its head to the end of its tail was a jagged mane of green triangles, sharp as swords and comprised of the same material from which its claws were made. From its bony arms hung huge black wings, with bulging dark red veins. The wings were each as large as its body, and the hands were attached to them.

The dragon had its eyes locked onto Jack who was now a helpless mortal prey below. With a sinister grin, it let out a piercing war cry. It was at this point (though only in retrospect would Jack realize it) that the dragon's terrifying demeanor was intended for one purpose and one purpose alone—paralysis of the victim by fear.

Sheer terror gripped Jack's heart as he stared back in horror at this terrible spectacle of evil. Thorn's throb suddenly jabbed him like a razor and shocked him out of the paralysis of fear that had begun to set in. He could now feel blood dripping from his wound.

With its high pitched, crackly voice, the dragon began to scream accusations against Jack, although he couldn't quite make out what exactly was being said. In the midst of all this horror, flaming arrows, projected out of the dragon's mouth, began to accompany each accusation. Each arrow, dripping with its own unique poison, was designed to have a potent effect on the central nervous system of its victim, causing the victim to believe the dragon's lies.

The fear of this beast had almost paralyzed Jack's mind—the very thing the dragon wanted so that his arrows would mortally penetrate his prey. But powerful adrenaline began to pour through him and his mind leapt into action. *Protection! I need protection! My shield! I need my shield!*

He had leaned his shield against the Chair of Rest and Truth before he sat down, and fortunately that was the one thing his hands could still reach. He grabbed the Shield of Faith just in time to block the immediate barrage of fiery arrows whistling toward him.

With a POP! Jack's ears opened and out of them flowed a green wax. Suddenly Jack began to clearly hear a loud debate. First he heard the dragon yelling all kinds of accusations and deceptions at him, but there was a stronger voice, coming from Jack's left, yelling back—no, roaring back!

Turning toward the other voice, Jack beheld a glorious terror! High up in a tree was a Warrior, a Champion without equal. He had fire in His eyes, and surrounding Him was the most brilliant light Jack had ever seen. Instantly Jack knew that this was the Son of the Father King. *This must be the One Azarel said had spilled His blood to make the Pathway of Faith.* He had heard Azarel talk much about Him, but even though Jack had never seen Him, he recognized Him. As paralyzing as the sight of the dragon was, this sight was exponentially more freeing. The light which exuded from His presence was a force that literally destroyed the deceptions of the dragon.

With each arrow of accusation fired from the dragon, the Son roared back a corresponding truth and out of His mouth would come a sword. The sword would not only knock down and destroy each of the flaming arrows, but would so brilliantly reflect the light of the Son that the dragon would become momentarily blinded.

Though these flaming arrows were flying all around him, their power seemed limited. When he kept his eyes on the Son and held up his shield, Jack noticed that all the arrows were quickly disarmed. But when he took his eyes off the Son, he had to fend for himself and the force of the arrows against his shield was practically unbearable.

The dragon had four basic arrows with a different false belief written on each one. After an arrow was shot, the dragon immediately unloaded a barrage of accusations against Jack, based on the false belief.

The first arrow had the word "Performance" written on it. This particular arrow was the most common of the four used against Jack, although it was the least penetrating. The flame accompanying this arrow was a moderately hot, fiery yellow-orange.

With it the dragon screamed, "You're a failure Jack! You've not measured up to the Father King's standards. You've let Him down, so you are worthless!" But afterwards, the voice of the Son came stronger, "No, Jack! You don't have to be perfect. Just believe in Me, and My love will free you from the need to perform!"

The second arrow had the word, "Approval" written on it. The impact of this arrow was stronger than the first, and as such, the corresponding flame had a hotter and more blazing orange-red hue.

After the dragon had shot this arrow, he immediately began to yell, "Jack, you're no good unless people approve of you! People tolerate you, Jack, but no one likes you—you are worthless and insignificant!" Against this arrow, the Son roared, "No, Jack! I alone am the Good One. It doesn't matter if the whole world rejects you. You are already totally accepted!"

"Blame" was written on the third arrow. The dragon only had a few of these, so they were used sparingly, but they were fashioned to penetrate deeply The flame on this arrow was a burning blue.

With this arrow, the dragon began to scream and cackle out a list of Jack's past failures: "You've ruined your life, Jack! You are unworthy of love or any good thing… and it's all your fault!" But against this arrow, the Son roared even louder, "No, Jack! I became failure, I took your blame. Your failure never condemns you! My love for you is completely secure!"

The last arrow was marked with the word, "Hopelessness." The impact of this arrow was so damaging that its prey rarely ever recovered if left to themselves. The flame corresponding to this arrow was the hottest of all flames—white.

With this arrow the dragon yelled, "You are what you are, Jack! You cannot change! You are hopeless! You are the result of your failures." But once again, against this last most deadly arrow came the loving, hope-filled words of the Son, "No, Jack! Believe in Me and know that you can rise above the past—I will empower you to do what you can't, and to become what you aren't!"

When Jack listened to the words of the Son, every arrow from the dragon's mouth was destroyed by the sword and disappeared in a puff of smoke. Whenever Jack listened to the words of the dragon, his arms grew tired; but when he listened to the words of the Son, he found a new surge of strength. In the midst of this ordeal, Jack realized that his Shield of Faith was enlarging as he used it.

Revelation finally dawned on Jack and the foolishness and futility of the dragon's words were suddenly exposed. He now saw through the lies that had plagued his entire life—lies that declared his worth was tied to his self-effort. In a moment, Jack understood how this belief kept him in bondage. The revelation caused him to suddenly break out in spontaneous worship, "Son, I love You! Father King, I trust You! Though You wound me, yet will I trust You! I know that Your words alone are the words of life!"

As the word "life" left Jack's mouth, the dragon instantly let out a blood curdling shriek of pain and covered its head with its claws and violently shook—as though its head were being crushed. With a mighty flapping of its wings the Accuser sprang from its perch, snapping branches and breaking treetops as it frantically flew away, screeching like a wounded animal.

After all this, Jack slumped over in his chair, drained and exhausted. Phobion appeared by his side, bandaged and black and blue. "Well, I guess we're safe for now," he whimpered as Jack slept. Little did he know there would be an even greater challenge that Jack would face in the Forest of Stillness.

Chapter Eight

FACING SOLUS

Maskon stood on Jack's shoulders, knocking him on the head with his fist. "Jack, wake up! Wake up!" Jack roused himself awake, but was disappointed that he was still tied to the chair. When he realized it was Maskon who awoke him, he became thoroughly irritated.

"Let me sleep, will you? Quit pestering me!"

"Jack, Jack, we've got to get out of here! He's coming, he's coming! I can hear him!" Maskon's eyes darted back and forth down the path.

"We're not going anywhere as long as I'm bound by these cords." Jack looked down dejectedly at the immovable rope securing him to the chair. "Anyway, what can be so frightening after that terrible dragon?"

"His eyes—I've heard that they're going to suck us in, and we'll feel a horrible sense of aloneness and have to face who we really are," Maskon cried and frantically looked around for something he could do to distract himself from the coming monster.

Solus was known as a Monster of Aloneness because he forced his victims to deal with a sense of being cut off from everyone and everything in the most horrible and painful of ways. Because of this, his victims would do all they could not to look into his eyes where his power resided.

"Oh, no, oh, no! I've never faced Solus. I've always run away! We're going to die!" Maskon was beside himself, pacing up and down in front of Jack.

Suddenly, through the trees came the sound of heavy pounding footsteps, along with the cracking and snapping of tree limbs and heavy breathing. With a loud roar, Solus crashed through the trees and onto the pathway directly in front of Jack. Maskon, trying to hide behind Jack's head, was gripping his hair and screaming. After just one look at the monster, Jack's heart froze in terror.

Essentially Solus looked like a ten foot tall, hunchbacked shadow. His shadowy-like quality made it difficult to make out too many details, except for his head which was the most solid part of him. His eyes were large sunken holes, appearing like the opening of a deep, dark cave, and his ears were quite large. He had a dinner plate sized hole for a mouth, out of which his words seemed to echo deeply and be accompanied by massive vibrations.

Frantically straining against the cords trying desperately to break away, Jack joined Maskon, screaming, "No! No! Go away! Leave me alone!" Then the hollow, base-sounding voice of Solus coldly intoned, "No, Jack, I will not go. I have come for *you*."

Solus moved closer and closer to Jack, until he bent down, breathed in his face and commanded, "Look into my eyes!"

"No! Never! I will not look!"

Turning his head back and forth, Jack avoided eye contact with Solus. Meanwhile, Maskon was being thrown back and forth as he continued to grip Jack's hair. On and on this went. Finally, Jack yelled out, "Help me, Creator! Help me! I can't do this anymore!"

Instantly, Maskon disappeared. In the midst of the terror came a loud BOOM! Solus covered his ears and fell to the ground completely limp, as though he were dead. Next came a powerful voice from heaven. Jack had heard this voice only once before when the Father King provided the bread and the water earlier in their journey. Nevertheless, Jack recognized His voice.

"Jack, you have embarked on the Journey of Honest Reckoning and vowed to be a seeker of Truth. My love for you can never be shaken. In My perfect love, there is no need to fear. Face what you have always feared. You will come to know My presence again, but only when you desire Me more than relief from your pain and terror. Aloneness can always be swallowed up in My love."

Then the Father King commanded, "Embrace him with your eyes, Jack! Embrace him now!"

With a divine surge of confidence, Jack forced himself to stare into the eyes of the hideous monster. In that same instant, Solus roared as he jumped up from the ground and hungrily locked his eyes onto Jack's. In a split second, each of his four dagger-hands pierced through Jack's hands and feet and pulled him into the monstrous body, right through those horrible vacuum eyes. The next instant, Jack found himself nailed down to a cross. This all happened just as quickly as Jack's confidence melted away into sheer terror. As he began to float down a tunnel, Jack felt an intense throbbing in his side—the pain of his Thorn. Suddenly, before his eyes flashed the words:

> *I have been crucified with Christ. It is no longer I who live, but Christ who lives in me. And the life which I now live in the flesh I live by faith in the Son of God who loved me and died for me.*

He had probably read those words at least 200 times before. He remembered doing word studies in Greek on them during his university years. Now, however, in his stance of total helplessness and surrender, the full extent of their meaning finally hit him.

The physical pain Jack felt was awful! Yet there was another more intense one that almost swallowed it up—the inward agony of absolute aloneness. This was a much more consuming pain stemming from the horrible realization of his true condition. Jack felt something black and ugly struggling and dying inside of him. Every fiber of his being felt the death pangs—especially his gut which responded in wrenching convulsions accompanied by a deep moaning. Tears streamed down his face.

Though swallowed up inside of Solus, Jack wasn't truly alone—there were others laid out all around him on crosses too. Jack noticed that many of them were frantically trying to pry themselves off their crosses. Some had succeeded, only to fall down into the eternal blackness that swallowed up their screams. Others, partially pried off, looked like they were the most miserable of all—halfway accepting their aloneness and halfway rebelling against it.

As Jack floated along, he became disillusioned, "I willingly submitted, but look! I am no different than anyone else—we're all nailed down. I don't understand."

Then in a peaceful breeze came a gentle voice, "Jack, trust Me. I AM all you need."

All of a sudden Jack realized that the "breeze" he felt wasn't wind but breath. Someone was behind him! He recognized the voice of perfect peace. Behind him was his Champion. The Son lay directly underneath Jack, and in the very same position. He too was crucified with the same nails and laying on His back against the wood. In all of this Jack began to find tremendous relief. Pure life literally seeped from the body of the Son.

Eventually, Jack felt pulses of life especially strong on one point of his back, directly behind his Thorn's throb, now growing acutely more painful in his side. Jack quickly recognized that the "pulse" he felt was coming from the Son. The Son, too, had a wound and it was bleeding. His side had been pierced and was throbbing. The vibrations went through Jack's back and right into his wound, eventually merging as one pulse.

Jack began to slowly realize that the pain of his Thorn was intimately connected with the suffering of the Son. It was as though the Thorn itself was a voice for the Son saying, "Embrace My sacrifice! Don't forget My blood! Rely only on Me!"

And so the wound of the Son released the pulse of life that Jack was experiencing on his cross—and in it all, such life was intimately connected with Jack's Thorn.

Sharing in the fellowship of His sufferings...that I might share in the power of His resurrection life pondered Jack as he recalled one of his favorite passages of Scripture. The reality of the Cross and the reality of Jack's Thorn were both taking on new powerful meanings.

On and on they floated as Jack was continually nourished by the presence of the Son. Occasionally Jack's focus would get off the presence of the Son and onto his desire to be out of the blackness. At this point, the pain of the Thorn would always return in sudden severity, and every time it was worse than before.

After such relapses, Jack would cry out for forgiveness for not focusing on the Son but allowing his circumstances to distract his mind and heart, he would then ease back into his internal posture of submission and embrace the cross. Again and again wonderful waves of heavenly peace would fill him to overflowing.

Jack could not believe the peace and contentment in which he had learned to abide. Somehow this stance of dependency seemed vaguely natural to him as though he had known it before. When was it? He knew it as a child, but he'd forgotten it many, many years ago...until now.

As the realization of Jack's dependency fully sank in, an explosion of light from the face of the Son not only lit up the darkness but actually transformed his surroundings. From the explosion of light, Solus seemed to somehow disintegrate into nothingness.

Suddenly, the blackness was gone, and so too were his deathly surroundings. Lying on his back and on the ground, Jack began to recognize the red bricks of the Pathway of Faith underneath him. He stood up and saw the Chair of Rest and Truth off to the side, but now the golden cords were limp on its seat.

The cross beneath Jack had actually become part of his own arms, legs, and backbone, an internalized living reality, reminding Jack of his crucified life in Christ and the safety and strength released to him from daily submission to his Lord.

All that visibly remained of the cross were thin brown lines running the length of Jack's arms, legs, and back, barely perceptible to the human eye, but they were there.

Jack stood looking at the Cords of Love and thought of the Son. He cried out, "Thank You, God, oh thank You for those precious cords!"

Then he once more started down the path, but now with more hope and joy than he had ever experienced before.

Chapter Nine

THE MOUNTAIN OF VISION

Leaving behind the Chair of Rest and Truth, Jack hiked several more miles until he emerged from the forest where Azarel was awaiting him.

"You wouldn't believe it! You wouldn't believe all that happened to me!"

"I saw it too, Jack, I was there. Remember, I told you I would be with you," Azarel said.

"It's so hard for me to believe you're present, Azarel, when I can't see or hear you."

"On this journey, faith is more important than seeing, hearing, or feeling—it is, in fact, their very substance."

"Azarel, I don't have that kind of faith—I'm stuck in my surface world of sensation and don't know how to break out."

"You have faith, Jack, but it is locked up within you, mostly through fear. There is only one way faith is released and one way alone."

"What's that?"

"You must listen to the words of the Father King. Come, you will learn more of this on the mountain."

"The Mountain of Vision?"

"Yes. We are almost there."

"Great! Let's go."

The travelers trekked on until a few hours later they arrived at yet another cabin. Just like the other one, it was completely prepared for them. Again they ate an enormous dinner and retired to their own rooms to enjoy a perfect night's rest. In the morning, as Jack and Azarel sat at the table, Jack was less than excited to eat what was set before him.

Instead of bacon and eggs, a thick, gray mealy porridge lay clumped in their bowls.

"What is this? It smells awful! Is there anything we can add to it? Sugar? Milk? Cinnamon?"

"No, Jack, you must learn to eat everything the Father gives you, just as He gives it to you, adding nothing. Though you may not like its taste, the Father has prepared it specifically for you. It is exactly what you need, though it may not be exactly what you like."

For the sake of obedience alone, Jack forced down his breakfast, trusting the truth of what he heard more than the argument of his tastebuds. After breakfast, they were soon on the road again and hiked for several hours until they arrived at the base of the Mountain of Vision around noon.

Azarel turned to Jack, "On the top of this mountain I will show you visions of truth regarding the painful Thorn in your side. Jack, you must understand that the Thorn is your friend. It drives you to find the healing truth, and it guards you from death's ruthless cohorts—complacency and denial."

In his mind Jack knew exactly what Azarel meant. This was the very thing he had recently experienced.

"This hike will take us about four hours, Jack, if we move right along. We will take periodic rests and eat as we need. The Father King has many types of fruit trees planted alongside the pathway to help nourish the hikers as they ascend the mountain. The fruits disturb the digestion of travelers who have wandered here on their own, but the breakfast you so disdained this morning will aid in your digestion and actually enhance the effects of the fruit so that you will continually feel strong."

Jack and Azarel spoke little on the ascent because the trail was often very tenuous, requiring their focused attention. They traveled over bridges, crossing rivers and streams; they followed riverside trails and hiked through meadows and pine groves. At times, the trail was level, but mostly it had a consistent incline all the while leading them directly up the mountain to the summit. Along the way they ate from a wide variety of fruits, some Jack recognized and many he didn't. They also had their heart's fill of all the cold, clear mountain water they could drink.

As they approached the summit, Jack asked, "Azarel, I need to discuss something with You—something I have found to be very frustrating, and I don't know what to do about it. I feel like I am living my life in isolation from everyone else. I feel like there is an invisible wall separating me from everybody and everything around me."

Jack paused to gather his thoughts, rubbed his forehead, and continued, "During these times I feel lonely and disconnected from the world. The experience robs me of experiencing life, as if all I can do is watch."

"Your problem is a problem with the eyes of your soul. Your soul has been in turmoil, Jack. You have tried to understand life with your physical eyes when it is only the eyes of the soul that can do it. We will talk more about this later, but look—we made it to the top!"

Azarel led Jack over to a rock-hewn ledge overlooking a beautiful valley, then came to a stop.

"Here you will experience the first vision of truth, Jack, and it is in response to the question you have just asked. Wait here, and the vision will speak."

Azarel left Jack alone with a breathtaking view before him. As he waited, the colors of the leaves seemed as though they were exploding right before his eyes. Everything was perfect…almost.

Jack felt that something was preventing him from fully experiencing this glorious moment. As beautiful as it was, he could not fully enjoy it.

In a few minutes, a huge thunderhead of black clouds rolled in, overshadowed the beautiful view, and settled over Jack.

Cleavon appeared crawling up Jack's leg, whimpering in fear. "Don't leave me, Jack. I'm afraid."

Then that awful cry came once again, and this time there was no mistaking that it truly was coming from Jack's own soul—he could even feel the vibrations in the center of his chest. Eventually they settled down to a moan—a weary sounding moan. Then the moan became words. Never before had Jack heard such a perfect expression of his feelings. The words that came forth were clear and distinct:

I am tired. I am worn.
Years have come. Years have gone.
Ceaseless striving since the day I was born.
Striving to live. Striving and torn.

So much thinking, so much feeling,
so much knowing.
Still, nothing gained…I live as a phantom flowing.
LIFE, YOU ESCAPE ME…
SELF, I KNOW YOU NOT!

Life's beauty found only in the glance,
Somehow disappears when sought in the stare.
Why do you mock me with your illusory dance?
Why can't I have you? Why can't I own you here?

Then I will live...then I will be.
OH GOD, SHOW ME LIFE!

First Vision—The Bubble

Instantly, the dark black clouds melted away as a rush of sunlight exploded through and rolled in over all the land.

As Jack stared out over the ledge, his eyes grew increasingly heavy, though he didn't feel tired. He closed them and instantly a vision flashed before the screen of his mind.

A bubble was softly floating over the face of the earth, gliding on the gentle currents of the wind. Glorious life continually surrounded its effervescent journey.

Jack looked closer and noticed that the bubble was a transparent shell, and in the shell was a man who looked miserable. In an instant, Jack recognized him—without a doubt, he knew it was himself. Finally the man opened his mouth and began to yell out in exasperation, "Help me, oh God! Free me from my prison!"

The bubble-shell continued to float across the sky, surrounded by the most beautiful scenery Jack had ever seen. With arms outstretched toward heaven, the man continued to scream to God for help. Outside the bubble not a soul could hear, save God Himself.

From heaven a whisper was heard, a whisper with the force of thunder. Instantly attentive, the man in the bubble dropped his hands, closed his mouth, raised his ear, and listened. These words, glistening in the glory of Omnipotence, burst forth:

> I have created life. I have established existence, even yours, as a marvelous thing. But I did not make your prison—you have created it. The moment you sought to own life is the moment you cut yourself off, for you are not the Creator, you are the creation. Live, not as unto yourself! Think, not as unto yourself! Feel, not as unto yourself! When you live unto yourself, you create a prison and shut yourself off from the abundant life I have for you. I say live! Live not unto yourself, but unto your Creator, amidst the chorus of creation I have set about you. Then you will truly live!

Now the vision abruptly changed. The prison shell was gone and the man was on the ground exuberantly dancing and singing. Filled with joy, he sang forth:

I am no longer tired, no longer worn.
Weariness is weakened; fatigue is gone.
Life is near; life is real; life is here!

No more staring, no more grasping, no more strife.
Selfishness consumed in the wonder of life.
Life is sweet; life is rich; life is complete!

Deception's false dream of life to own,
Utterly shattered—real treasure now shown.
With hands lifted up in praise,
Thank God, my prison is razed!

The vision faded away, Jack opened his eyes and Azarel put his hand on his shoulder. "This is where the Creator wants to bring you, Jack—into perfect harmony with Him and the creation He has made. This is what the Journey of Honest Reckoning is all about. Life can never be owned; it can only be experienced. It is like the wind—you can't hold it, you can only experience it. When you seek to grab hold of life, immediately the shell is formed and you remain on the inside looking out. Only when you learn to give your life away do you learn how to find it. It is toward this reality that the Pathway of Faith is leading you, and it is toward this aim that Thorn's Prod is bringing you."

"Azarel, how could someone possibly know me that well? The voice spoke exactly what I felt."

With a finger pressed against his lips, Azarel whispered, "We must go. If we tarry, we will miss the next vision."

Second Vision—The Holes of Creation

Leaving the rocky ledge, the two made their way down into a nearby thick forest and onto a soft rug of pine needles in the midst of a wide clearing.

"Sit down. It is time for you to see the second Vision of Truth," said Azarel, motioning Jack to a nearby rock. He looked deeply into Jack's eyes as he continued, "All of creation is horribly sick with a deadly disease—eating holes into its very own soul. Like one crippled by arthritis, creation grows into an inwardly bent posture from trying to heal and fix itself, all the while refusing to straighten out and hear the healing word from the Creator above. Shhh…be still and listen."

Azarel disappeared into the silence. Alone on the rock, Jack felt the forest closing in on him—an illusion the descending mist gave him.

The pain in his side suddenly flared up, and blood began to drip. Then rising into a crescendo of agony, Thorn's Cry filled the atmosphere and echoed through the trees as though it were telling everything to be quiet and listen.

The cry stopped. Jack had a sense of foreboding as panic began to close in on his neck, making it hard to breathe.

"Jack, Jack, what are you going to do?" whined Cleavon, suddenly appearing on Jack's shoulder, grabbing his shirt around his neck and pulling tighter and tighter. "You know you can't live in this stillness forever. Jack, you need a companion—you need a wife. You need to get married soon—your fiancée will dress your wound; she will heal you."

A thick gray mist fell over the forest just as Cleavon disappeared. An approaching man and woman could be faintly seen walking in the heavy mist toward Jack. As they got closer, Jack could see that their heads were hanging down as if in some grave sorrow. A slight breeze blew away the mist and the image became clear.

Both stopped. The man took one more step forward, lifted his head and his torn shirt exposed a huge disease-ridden hole covering his abdomen. Jack winced at the grotesque scene.

The man spoke:

There's a hole in my soul.
I thought I could fill it;
Still it is empty and void.

There's loneliness in my soul.
There's sorrow in my soul.
Perhaps I can fix it;
Maybe it isn't so bad.

There's a hole in my soul.
There's sickness in my soul.
I am in pain.
There's a hole in my soul,
Why can't I fix it?

He then looked to the woman and extended his hand. She raised her head and looked over to him. In a hopeful look, the man said, "Maybe you can heal me." Then suddenly he gasped, "No, look! You too have sickness in your soul!" Her blouse was torn at the bottom, revealing the same cancerous hole in her body. As he reached toward her she vanished. Gripping his side, the man fell in pain onto his knees. Then out of his mouth came Thorn's cry. Instantly Jack's side began to vibrate in harmony with the wail. It was then that Jack realized he was once again watching himself.

Suddenly flashing over him were a multitude of images—cars, money, honors, and achievements.

The images disappeared and silence fell. The man looked up to see a scattered multitude of people suddenly materialize around him. All the people were crunched over, holding their sides. Yet strangely, on each and every face could not be found a single sentiment of pain or anguish. Instead they wore brazen grins of denial.

Maskon suddenly appeared, quite pleased at this turn of events. "See, Jack. They can do it and so can you. None of this worrying about that pain. It's probably all in your head anyway."

Then the multitude raised their voices into a chorus of protest.

Ignore the hole!
There is no hole!
There is nothing to fix!

The man, still gripping his side, lifted his head and cried out, "No, No, No! It *is* real! Can't you see? The hole is real!"

The voice of the multitude quieted and, as Maskon faded away in confusion, the man continued to reflect, though now with great frustration:

There are holes in our souls,
Creation has holes,
All creatures are bent,
And miserably like it!

Above him the trees opened up and the gathered clouds pulled apart. In a brilliant explosion of color he saw a majestic throne—colors of red, gold, purple, and yellow reflected off its massive surface, while around it were rainbows of every imaginable color. On the throne was the Creator Himself. He looked down with arms outstretched and said, "COME!"

The man immediately stood up and raised his arms, along with many others from the multitude who had been crunched over and looked upward. With newness of life, they cried out, "We can see! The veil is lifted! We are sick, we are broken, but You bring healing and You bring health. You are LIFE! We are Yours!"

Then the entire multitude vanished except the man still gazing at the Creator. In erupting worship, he burst forth:

There's a hole in my soul…
But You make me whole.

The hole remains,
But You always fill it.

There's a hole in my soul...
BUT YOU MAKE ME WHOLE!

Then the man vanished into the mist. A few moments later, the sound of footsteps in the leaves and the familiar voice of Azarel approached.

"Never forget the lesson you have seen, Jack. Nothing but the Creator can fill that vast hole in your soul. No woman, no job, no form of power, nothing but the Father Himself can fill it. The wail you hear is the cry of humanity mourning the cancerous condition of creation—the cry of brokenness realized. Creation knows that something is terribly wrong, in spite of the fact that it has learned to close its eyes and deny this truth. Creation is powerless to change itself. Jack, the hole will remain until the day when the new creation invades the old. The Creator is the only One who can fill the holes. Nothing or no one else can ever fill it."

In saying those last words, Azarel came in front of Jack and, with his finger pointed, struck him just under his heart right on the tender spot of his Thorn.

"Oww!" said Jack, as he grabbed his side and wiped away some blood.

Azarel then, taking the same finger, again touched the wound, and it stopped bleeding.

"Never forget your Thorn, Jack, and never forget your Healer."

Third Vision—The Runner

"We must head toward the third and final vision. Come," said Azarel as he moved on.

They left the forest and walked back to the rocky ledge, all the way over to the far side of the summit which ended at an abrupt ridge. Here nature's balcony overlooked a magnificent valley—heaven's beauty spilled out on the expanse below. Bordering this glorious picture was the ocean itself, crashing onto the broad sandy beach below.

"Listen and watch," Azarel said as he left.

Jack stood basking in the beauty, fully enjoying the sun's warmth, the beauty below, and the colorful brilliance of light. Then, like a gradual awakening from a peaceful sleep, Jack became distracted by an uncomfortable, anxious feeling on his chest. Soon the feeling gave way to physical poking as Maskon appeared with Professor Gnosis.

"Jack, Jack!" they yelled.

"Why do you keep bothering me?"

Maskon began, "Yeah, well, it's so quiet up here, so still, you need to be doing something, Jack. This journey has made you too lazy. You never used to be this way before. Don't you feel like running away from this absurd stillness?"

"That's right," piped in Professor Gnosis. "You know you're never going to find that 'one thing' just sitting around. Research it out, I always say. You are sure to find your answers in books. Use your mind, son, that's why you've got it. You're intelligent enough to figure it out."

Maskon interrupted, "And there are lots of things you need to do when you get back home. When these things are accomplished, you will have reason to feel good about yourself and about your life. When you finally get married and receive that promotion, then you can rest! Then you'll really enjoy life."

Upon hearing all the noise, Azarel returned and was very angry. He walked toward the elves, pointed at them, and commanded, "Quiet! Stop your disturbance!" Then He turned to Jack and quietly asked, "Why do you put up with them? You are the one that has the power of choice."

Silence followed and the characters quickly disappeared as Azarel left once again.

Jack began to hear yet again the Cry—only now it was faint and dull. Looking down on the beach, he saw a man. As he looked, the third and final vision began to unfold. The man was wearing a ragged shirt with the letters J.A. unmistakably written on it. The man strangely resembled a wild stallion irresistibly running the ocean beaches, unable to be still, unable to rest.

Pondering all of this, Jack was painfully struck with the meaning—he was viewing the state of his own soul. *Striving. Striving. Striving. My life has been a futile attempt, a hopeless reach for perfection. My religion is powerless...its source was only me. My loneliness and frustration are unbearable. I've fooled the world and tried to fool myself. I thought my efforts would win me life; instead, my efforts have been only a miserable chasing of the wind.*

The scene changed—no longer was the man crazed and ragged looking, and no more was he running at the ocean. Instead he now ran at the site of an Olympic track. He was running hard, really hard, thinking his opponents were far behind. Finally, he glanced down and was aghast to see that he was only running on a treadmill, going nowhere! In frustration and exhaustion, he collapsed onto the ground. He saw that he was only at the starting line of the track and the race had not yet even begun. All his running was in vain! Then he looked up at the starting line and saw a woman with the words "Ex-prostitute" instead of a number on the front of her running outfit, poised to begin the race. To her left was a man with the words "Ex-drug addict" on his shirt.

How can this be? It isn't fair. I lived a life of sacrifice in moral purity and sinful restraint. Yet, they never withheld an earthly lust from their mouths or hands. Now look! They're both in better positions than I am!

The runner dropped his head into his hands and exclaimed, "These pitiful souls are in a better starting position than I am. They have found out before me that any selfish efforts to grab and get life end up utterly futile... even my own self-righteous efforts."

Far up on the ledge Jack was wiping fresh blood from his side. Just then the runners looked up at Jack viewing the vision. Jack froze. No longer was he viewing the vision, the vision was viewing him!

The ex-drug addict said, "Why have you tried to finish in your own strength what has already begun as a gracious resource of the Spirit?" Then the ex-prostitute, with tears in her eyes, pleaded, "Don't you see, Jack, that your self-righteousness was no better than our self-indulgence? The race is not to the swift or strong but to those who endure only by the grace of God's goodness and power, not the swiftness or strength of our efforts."

As the image faded away, Jack cried out in grief, "So what do I get for all my righteous efforts? A proud heart! I'm no less sinful than either of these."

Standing up, and facing the edge of the cliff, Jack screamed out, "Oh, pitiful pride! You have blinded many eyes to the truth! Be gone! You will fool me no more! All are sinners! All are helpless! All need Father King's grace! All need His mercy!"

Jack fell to his knees and began to sob, then wail. At this point Azarel walked over and touched his shoulder, and said, "Jack, the truth hurts, but without such pain there is no healing, and without such grief there is no real repentance and change. Know that a broken and contrite heart the Father will never turn away. Hide these truths in your heart, ponder and dwell on them. They were given specially for you. Never run from the pain of honest truth, but learn to embrace it. There you will see your pain turned to joy and peace."

Jack had no desire to speak since he was keenly feeling the pain of truth's revelation and the embarrassment of being so exposed.

"Jack, it's been a full and long day. It is important for you to rest, and I am going to take you to the perfect place."

"Where?"

"To an elderly couple assigned by the Father King to serve all, who, like yourself, have been exposed and cut by the truths of the Mountain of Vision. Their job is to serve you in whatever way you need."

"That's fine Azarel, but I don't feel like talking to anyone tonight."

"Jack, the Father King knows exactly what you need. He has already informed our hosts and they have made appropriate preparations. They reside there specifically to serve all pilgrims like yourself."

Azarel led Jack to the cabin, which was only a short distance away. This one was similar to the others except that it was twice as large.

They walked up the stone pathway to wooden steps leading to a wide porch that wrapped all the way around the house. The view from the porch overlooked the ocean and was breathtakingly beautiful.

The woman greeted Jack and Azarel. "Hello, Azarel. It is good to see you again—always a treat."

"Don't worry about me, I know the process. I will stay out of the way and allow you to do your job."

They both smiled as Azarel waved and walked to a railing overlooking the ocean. No words needed to be spoken, a shared "silent knowing" had been forged over the years between this couple and Azarel. He had led thousands of similar pilgrims to these unequaled servants of the Father King.

The woman looked to be probably in her 80s. Her smile, wrinkled face, and gray hair made her look like a seasoned grandmother. She held out a welcoming hand to Jack. "Welcome, Jack Avery. We are here to serve you. This is a house of silence tonight because that is what Father King said you needed most. There is a hot bath waiting for you. It has been prepared with a special ointment to treat your wound. Afterwards, we will serve you dinner in silence, unless you choose to speak. After you have eaten your fill, you may go to your room and sleep for as long as you like. We are at your service for anything else you desire."

Jack felt safe and cared for in this house. The husband didn't say a word. He just had a twinkle in his eye and slight grin that made Jack know that it was okay for him to be recovering, and that he didn't have to try and be perfect. The man had a look of understanding, so Jack deduced that he had probably at one time had a similar experience himself.

From this point on, the night was a blur for Jack—there was a bath and then a large dinner with chicken and gravy and fresh picked vegetables. The next thing he remembered was waking up to breakfast in his room—cereal, yogurt, toast, and eggs. Jack was so grateful that the breakfast wasn't like the last one.

When breakfast was over, Jack relaxed in another hot bath, after which he was thoroughly refreshed. As he finished dressing, Azarel entered the room.

"How do you feel, Jack?"

"Very good. I slept great. The Father King knew exactly what I needed."

"He always does, Jack, He always does. We just need to trust Him."

"That, I am learning."

After they thanked the elderly couple and said goodbye, the travelers began their journey back down the mountain.

Chapter Ten

THE RAFT OF FREEDOM

"We're not going back down the same way we came," Azarel explained, as they continued on their journey. "Those who travel the Pathway of Faith learn that every step, every mile traveled is new and fresh, so one's journey never requires them to repeat the steps of their past. In the Kingdom of the Father, the steps of the past are done away with; lessons may be repeated, but the path is always new."

"Where are we going next?" Jack asked.

"Remember the ocean you saw from the mountain?"

"How could I forget? It was a breathtaking view!"

"That is where we're going."

"Fantastic!"

As they hiked down the mountain, Jack noticed another stand of poles lining the path, just like those he had seen with Everyman. Some poles were decorated with masks while others were empty.

Answering Jack's questioning look, Azarel explained,

"These masks represent the three types of deception you just learned about on top of the mountain—seeking to own life, seeking to fill one's holes of need, and self-righteousness. Remember? Those who refused the truths you have learned have acquired such masks, as you can see," said Azarel pointing to the poles with empty spaces for the masks.

By afternoon, they had arrived at the bottom of the mountain and followed the trail out of the woods to the sandy beach. At the top of a sand dune, they saw a small raft chained around a huge stake in the sand.

"This is what you will travel in," Azarel said, "the Raft of Freedom."

"In that? It's so...so small. Where are we going? How can you call that little thing the 'Raft of Freedom?'"

"Jack, you must trust the Father King. It is time for you to face your fear of death. He wants to show you that His comfort is more powerful than any fear you could ever face. The Father King wants to demonstrate His providence and protection over your life and help you enjoy the freedom you have always desired. Are you willing to trust Him?"

Instantly all the characters materialized—Maskon, Cleavon, Gnosis, and Phobion all began to shout at once, "No Jack! No! Don't go! You'll never survive! We'll all drown."

Jack looked at Azarel.

"Jack, has the Father King once let you down on this journey? Can you trust Him or not?"

Jack nodded his head and then hushed the elves as he unchained the raft and dragged it down to the water. He climbed into the raft and looked back at Azarel still standing on the beach.

"Aren't you coming?"

"Jack, you are learning to trust the Father. I will be with you; but as before, you will not see or hear me."

After Azarel shoved the boat into the water and away from the shoreline, the elves faded away. As the wind began to blow the raft out to sea, a wave of fear rolled over Jack as Thorn's Prod began to pound.

He shook it off, grabbed the oars and began to row while praying that the Father King would show him what to do and where to go. After an hour of rowing, Jack was far out into the water and could only faintly see the land. For the next hour, he rowed even harder because of all the nervous energy bursting through his body.

As night approached, Jack's arms began to ache, and he began to more fully realize the reality of his situation. Phobion popped up on his left and began jabbering at him.

"Jack, for heaven's sake, it's pitch dark with choppy waves all around us. I told you not to head out into who knows where. Now look at the fix you've got us into."

The wind picked up speed, and Jack's heart began to race. Minutes felt like hours and hours like days. The thought of remaining stuck on a little raft all night sent shivers of panic and terror up and down Jack's spine.

Maskon was sitting on his shoulder, holding on for dear life. "Jack, we're in the middle of the ocean and you don't even know which way to row! This doesn't look good. You can't just sit there. Do something! Do anything!"

Jack was now overwhelmed with fear of the waves capsizing the raft and the possibility of sharks in the water.

Meanwhile, Phobion had slid down to the bottom of

the raft. He stood there awkwardly squirming and anxiously tapping his foot. Jack's foot soon began tapping and fell in sync with the elf's rhythm. Phobion had a wide-eyed, glazed over look and monotonously repeated, "What next, Jack? What next?"

Finally, the wind died down, almost to nothing. As Jack floated aimlessly in the dark, it occurred to him that his fear of death was really a symptom of a deeper fear—one he had never before recognized—the fear of losing control over his life. He had to admit that death was the ultimate example of it. This fear that had terrorized Jack all his life.

He felt naked and completely insecure. He had no way to protect himself. He was totally at the mercy of the deep and the power of the elements. The pounding of Thorn's Prod had now become like the poking of a knife.

After sitting hour after hour in the inky blackness, Jack realized that something unusual began to happen—his senses were growing increasingly keener. He became aware of non-physical things in a way he had never been before. The eyes of his soul were unveiled to see the illusion we call control. Jack became increasingly aware of a reality of life that his busyness had always kept him distracted from—the reality of the spirit.

He had learned to place so much importance on his physical world, expecting it to ultimately protect and sustain his life, that he never could get a clear view of the spiritual world. Now that he was looking at the world with spiritual eyes, the superficial surface world of the physical crumbled in front of him. Suddenly Jack became fully aware of this other reality of life he had never much noticed before.

Spiritually, Jack was passing through a doorway from where he could glimpse the spiritual foundation upon which the physical world is displayed and sustained. He was learning a new frame of reference which had so long been hidden to him.

At first, he enjoyed this new sense of the spiritual. But when nothing happened hour after hour, he grew impatient. Phobion chattered endlessly about their dire situation. The raft rocked back and forth, back and forth on the waters, as the night ruthlessly dragged on and on. When daylight came, there was no relief in sight. He could not glimpse land in any direction, so he abandoned any efforts of rowing. He knew it was useless. True to Azarel's word, provision was always there for him. Food and water were no problem because there was a special canteen of water and a loaf of bread that never ran out. The only instructions left for him were: "Eat and drink only what you need, and trust for the rest."

The endless drifting and seeming hopelessness of the next two days became a living nightmare for him. Jack tried to distract himself from Phobion's incessant whining by making his mind focus on any possible topic other than his present situation. The intensity of effort to maintain this state of mental distraction finally ended in his complete physical exhaustion.

It was on the third day when Jack's terror finally reached its pinnacle. He threw himself face down on the raft and began to scream out, "I can't take it any more! Help me, God, or I will die!" Jack lay there uncontrollably sobbing.

The puddle of tears under him was soon mixed with Thorn's blood now dripping from Jack's side. In a mysterious way, Jack noticed that his tears brought him a feeling of solace. Slowly his tears of despair turned into tears of thankfulness and peaceful contentment. Eventually, like a refreshing mist, peace slowly rose up from the depths of his soul.

As the unveiling reached its greatest heights, Jack realized that all humanity was out of control and totally helpless.

Gnosis couldn't stand it any more and popped up on his back. "Jack, don't be a fool! If we can't control ourselves, who can? From all your studies, you know that…"

Jack screamed, "Quiet! Now I know the truth—control is just an illusion! Only a fool would believe it exists."

At this proclamation, something deep in Jack's chest seemed to shift and drop into a position that made him feel secure, or more precisely, anchored. Gnosis immediately disappeared.

Silence. Stillness. He knew this place. He had been there many times before on this journey. It was the Place of Broken Desperation, a total ceasing of all restless activity and expectations. How quickly he had forgotten. Jack became excited as he again discovered this place of faith—the place of confidence and security through letting go.

On the one hand something had just transpired, something spiritual had just happened. Whether it was in Jack or outside of him, he didn't know. But on the other hand, nothing had physically changed. Absolutely nothing! He knew both were true—nothing had changed, but everything was different. The only thing that had changed was that Jack had surrendered in an area he had never before surrendered—the fear of death and the need to control his life. He was finally free!

Rolling over onto his back with arms flung outstretched toward heaven, Jack felt joy and contentment as never before. He lay there and laughed and laughed and laughed, finally released from the fear of having to control his life. Jack was free!

At this exact moment, the wind shifted and began to blow the raft toward land that slowly appeared on the horizon. The wind picked up in speed and Jack's raft skipped across the water, heading inland as though there were a sail connected to it.

Sitting in his raft, Jack was totally at peace. He drank in the refreshing peace for hours as he slowly headed back toward the shore. Jack's raft, though once a place of fear, had now become a home of peace and freedom. Toward the end of the voyage, Jack was so struck with the love and goodness of the Father King that he became overcome with happiness, so much so that he could do nothing other than laugh once more.

Jack was so caught up in his joy that he didn't even notice the raft rapidly approaching the beach. He was all the more drunk with giddiness when a wave close to the beach capsized the raft and left him on his hands and knees in the shallow ocean surf.

Pulling himself out of the water, Jack stepped lightly up the sandy beach. Behind him, a familiar voice said, "Hey, give me a hand with this raft!"

Jack looked back to see Azarel grinning. Straining to pull the raft ashore, Azarel said, "I told you I'd be with you!"

Chapter Eleven

THE VALLEY OF THE SHADOW OF DEATH

After pulling the raft out of the water, Jack and Azarel dragged it up the sand dune and tied it back to the stake.

"You're learning much on this journey, aren't you Jack?"

"Too much. I could never do all the things I'm learning."

"You are right, you will never be able to do all these things, but you've also been learning that you don't have to—that's the beauty of being the Father's son, Jack. The Father does what we are not able to, and in the process, changes us to do what we could never do before. You are never alone, Jack. The Son has promised to be with all the sons and daughters of the Father. As you learn to walk in this new mindset, you will know His power and presence more and more each day. The secret is to learn to walk in the posture of grace."

"What do you mean the posture of grace?"

"It's the exact opposite of pride. It is the posture of humility and divine dependency, of learning in your heart how to spiritually walk on your knees all day long."

"Azarel, you know, I think I'm learning how to live all over again. Before I only knew how to *exist*, but now I am learning how to *live*, and it's wonderful!"

"Yes, Jack, it *is* wonderful, but you have also learned that this life is not without cost. Only as you give your life away to the Father do you receive it back in the greatest measure."

"Oh, yes, even if it costs me everything, I'd gladly give it all!"

"Jack, you say that so quickly. Do you really know what that means?"

"Yes, absolutely, Azarel! I would gladly give my life to have the life of the Father King in me."

"Yes, you will. You will give all, and you will suffer greatly; but in the end, you will receive far more than what you gave."

On and on, Azarel and Jack talked as they moved off the beach and back on the trail, which slowly began a gradual ascent. Finally they came to a wooden sign along the side of the path. On it were the words:

There is a river whose streams make glad
the city of God, the holy place
where the Most High dwells.

"What does it mean?" Jack asked.

"It means that we are almost at the doors of the Kingdom. Listen," said Azarel. "Do you hear the sound of the roaring water?"

Jack cupped his ears with his hands and listened. It sounded like a faint wind tunnel. "Yes, I hear it."

"What you hear is the River of Life, and it is that which shall lead us to the Kingdom."

"I don't understand," said Jack.

"The river is what supplies life to all the inhabitants—it flows directly to the gates of the city. When the Son was here on earth, He spoke of this river. He said if anyone was thirsty, He would give them rivers of living water. He gives life to all who believe on Him, and they will never thirst again. The river is our source of life. In order to find the Kingdom, we must first find the life, for the Father King has decreed that no one comes to the Kingdom but through the Son."

"I can hardly wait to get there!"

"Jack, you must know that this River of Life comes only with great cost. Only after one has experienced death does one experience the river. Death must precede life. Jack, you can have the life you seek, but to do so you must learn to submit yourself to death—the dying of all that is not pure within. The life of the Son is resurrection life, and such life does not come to that which is alive, but only that which has already died. Jack, your Thorn is your reminder of brokenness. As you embrace it, you embrace death, but in the embrace, life is birthed. In this way alone is the Kingdom discovered. The way of the Thorn is the way to the Kingdom. The price of such eternal life while here on earth is to enter into a living death now."

"Is this what I experienced inside of Solus?"

"Yes, that is precisely what I mean. As you learned to no longer be afraid of aloneness and the inadequacy of your soul to break free of this reality, you then learned to experience the One who promised never to leave nor forsake you. In Him, you found comfort.

"Here you will face death by recognizing not only the inadequacies of your soul but also the inadequacies of your body to continually release life. Your body will soon meet its limit. Here, you will face the physical reality of your mortality.

"In Solus you learned how to offer your soul as a living sacrifice; here you will learn how to offer your body as a living sacrifice. If you want life, Jack, you must first learn to embrace death."

At a curve in the Pathway of Faith, Azarel stretched out his hand, "Look over there."

Over to the left where the forest ended and the path could be seen to continue, Jack saw a barren valley opening up before them. "I've never seen anything so dismal in all my life. Everything looks dead!"

The valley was worse than a desert—it was a scorched wasteland. Every bit of moisture had been fully extracted from the ground by the heat of the sun, leaving only a jagged pattern of cracks and ridges where the earth had pulled apart from itself. The ground was mostly grayish brown, but it was black in places where fire had completely devoured the underbrush. Bare tree trunks sporadically were scattered all the way to the next mountain and stood pointing up to the sky. Each one was scorched black with its charred limbs partly visible in the ashes heaped around its base. Nothing looked alive in this wasteland—riverbeds were dried up, and their empty bottoms revealed rocks and boulders all atop a gray sandy top layer.

Looking at the desolation, Jack shook his head. "What happened here?"

"Death. The Father King declared that nothing should live in this place. He sent His servants to cut off the river's source and put fire to all the land so that the testimony would remain that nothing lives without the River of Life. That is where we're headed. It's called The Valley of the Shadow of Death. In this valley, however, we will find the River of Life."

"We're going down there?" Phobion could be seen whispering in Jack's ear until Jack swatted at him like one does at a pesky fly.

"Yes, remember death must precede life, Jack. Don't doubt but believe."

The skepticism on Jack's face changed to determination as he appeared to make a decision. "Okay, I choose to believe."

Completely disregarding Jack's statement of faith, Phobion decided to make one more attempt at convincing Jack to take another path. He called on Gnosis to help him. Standing sternly on top of Jack's head, Gnosis began to tap, tap, tap on it.

"Jack, you don't have to go through that horrible place, you know. Remember when Azarel left you in that boat for all those days? Well, you want to make a bet that he waited on the beach munching pineapples and coconuts while you suffered on bread and water? Now he probably knows a shortcut around this desert, and as soon as your back is turned, he'll take it. You're too smart for this. Ask him for a map or something so we can figure out a better way around this horrid valley..."

Before Gnosis got any further, Jack held up his hand to stop him. He paused and swallowed, feeling a large knot in his throat, then quietly said, "The Father King has proved His goodness. I have no reason to doubt Him now."

Azarel solemnly nodded and together they hiked down to the valley until they came to an ominous sign that read:

Welcome to the Valley
of the Shadow of Death.

Azarel put his arm on Jack's shoulder. "Jack, every one who enters this valley must be convinced of one thing if he or she is to survive—the unshakable certainty of the goodness of God. Only the ones who have such assurance are the ones able to abandon their lives to His care. Are you convinced of this, Jack?"

Without hesitation this time, Jack said, "Yes, I am."

"Jack, in the raft you learned how to find freedom from your fear of death. Here, the Father King wants to take you even further. He is going to teach you how to actually *embrace* death. You won't fully understand it now, but you will later. This will be the greatest test you have yet faced on this journey."

Jack felt fear and faith at the same time—fear was in his head, but faith was strong in his heart.

As they followed the path into the valley, Jack felt like he was walking into a fiery furnace. He shuddered as the hot air filled his lungs, forcing him to pause before he could exhale and move forward again. It was so hot and so dry that it wasn't very long before he felt completely fatigued.

"Azarel, I can't keep going without water."

"There is no water here."

"But what about the river?"

"The river only comes after death. Jack, you are walking the Walk of Death right now. You must trust the Father King to bring you through it. Continue walking and never stop trusting Him for every step."

"I will trust, if He will help me."

"He always does, Jack, He always does."

On they walked and walked and walked. By the middle of the day, Jack was dragging his feet over the sand. The effect of the glaring sun had taken its toll on him—his face, head, neck, and arms were thoroughly scorched, and his lips were swollen and cracked. He stumbled now and then, and every few steps Jack would muster just enough strength to mumble, "I-I-I-I… t-t-t-r-ru-u-s-st… You-u-u… Fa-a-a-th-h-her-r."

Finally, Jack collapsed face down on a mound of dirt that in his dazed condition seemed to appear to look like an altar. As he lay there, Phobion started shaking him, "It's not supposed to end this way, Jack!"

Maskon appeared and looked desperate. He took off his hat and paced up and down Jack's prone body. "Jack, come on, you'll make it! What would people think if you ended up this way? Come on, man. The show must go on! You can do it."

"I can do…nothing," Jack whispered.

Just as he began to slip out of consciousness, Jack felt a trickle of water flowing across his lips. Then it grew and grew into a puddle…suddenly, out of the puddle exploded an immense geyser that showered water all over him. The water instantly revitalized Jack, healed his scorched skin, brought his lips back to normal, and filled him with strength. Getting to his feet, Jack saw Azarel by his side with a huge grin on his face.

"Jack, only the Father can make streams in the wasteland."

As Azarel was speaking, the ground began to rumble, and then with a massive jolt the earth suddenly split wide open all down the length of the desert. The water gushed up from the ground and began to fill it until soon it became a tremendous river.

"Jack, the River of Life!"

"This is amazing!" Jack raised his hands toward heaven and shouted and cried with joy.

"Jack! Are you still convinced of the goodness of God?" Azarel yelled over the roaring of the river.

"How could I not be?"

"Are you sure?"

"Yes! Why?"

"Then jump in! This is the only way to the Kingdom!"

Jack stopped short in his rejoicing and looked carefully at the raging river. "In that? Are you serious? I'm not a strong swimmer at all!"

"Jack, in this river, you could only drown from life. There is no death!"

As Azarel was shouting out these last words, he backed up a few steps and ran forward, took a flying leap, and landed in the river. Before he was quickly swept out of sight, he yelled up to Jack, "Just believe! I'll see you ther-r-r-r-r-r-re!"

Jack stood on the bank, staring at the swiftly flowing river. He knew in his heart that he was prepared to jump, but he still hesitated. Finally he gathered enough courage and got into position to begin his run.

Suddenly a barrage of resistance met him, as the elves materialized.

"Wait! Wait! Don't jump in!" Phobion screamed.

Cleavon held onto both Jack's legs as if to prevent him from running. "Don't leave us, Jack. We need you."

Looking down at a piece of paper, Gnosis said, "I can't find this river on my map anywhere. Maybe you can hike along the bank and follow the river to the Kingdom, or perhaps it's less rough farther down. Yes, I do believe that would be the wise choice."

For a split second, Jack began to question his decision. Then instantly Azarel's words flashed across his mind: "Just believe, Jack!"

With that final encouragement, Jack made up his mind and began to sprint toward the bank. All the while Maskon was bug-eyed in terror, Phobion was chomping on his fingernails, Professor Gnosis had fainted, and Cleavon, as always, was gripping even tighter onto Jack's leg.

All the elves disappeared in fright as Jack leapt into the roaring water. His fear found instant release in a divine rush of freedom and joy. He laughed joyously as the river effortlessly carried him away from the desolate wasteland.

PART II

THE MARKING OF THE THORN

Chapter Twelve

THE KINGDOM DISCOVERED

Carried along in the holy current of liquid love, Jack was undone. His emotions of pure joy drove him to alternate between laughing, crying, and singing. Never before had he so intensely felt the love of the Father King.

The River of Life eventually slowed down to a shallow stream, and he tumbled onto the soft riverbank. He slowly sat up to get his bearings as he dried off in the bright sun.

As the intensity of his emotions slowly faded, he became more aware of his surroundings. Just up the hill, Jack recognized the continuation of the Pathway of Faith. When he climbed up to it, he saw that it unrolled into a beautiful meadow spread out before him as far as he could see on either side. The meadow was in full bloom with wildflowers of exquisite variety and beautiful fragrance.

Jack looked around in confusion. His wild emotional ride down the river had not prepared him for this serene place. Although it was beautiful, he was somewhat disappointed. Azarel had told him that the river would lead him straight to the gates of the Kingdom, but here he saw no gates, only acres and acres of peaceful landscape.

Professor Gnosis started pulling on his collar. "Jack, see I told you. You didn't use your head and follow my directions. No, you had to dive headlong into that raging river. Now where has it gotten you? To a field of flowers, although it is pretty, I must admit. But what are you going to do? There's no purpose for you here."

Maskon appeared on his shoulder. "Yes, Jack. What are you going to do here? There's no one around within miles. I'm glad you didn't give up back there—some performance, pal! But hey, maybe now you'll realize it's all up to you to make it here. Stop listening to that Azarel. Ever since you met up with him, all you've had is trouble."

Down on his leg, Cleavon said, "Jack, please let's go back home. You need Julie. She's the one that can make you feel complete. Let's go back."

The one thought Jack had refused to entertain this entire journey now began to finally surface: "Maybe there really isn't a Kingdom. Perhaps my hopes were too good to be true."

Suddenly, a silent flash of light shot across the meadow. And then another and another. Each flash drew his vision to a point somewhere off in the distance.

Jack's eyes widened as he gasped in excitement.

Hope began to rise in his heart. Off in the distance he saw something, although he wasn't sure if it might be a hallucination or some figment of his imagination. But the more he focused, the more he could unmistakably tell just what it was. He gasped as the realization hit him—he was getting his first glimpse of the Kingdom. He couldn't help himself, he began to run toward it, leaving the elves to fade away. The closer he got, the more amazed he was—the Kingdom was astoundingly magnificent although Jack was still too far away from it to see most of the details.

Overcome with excitement, Jack began to shout, "The Kingdom! The Kingdom! I found it. I really found it!"

Flinging his arms, and wildly shouting with joy, Jack was overcome with happiness at his long-awaited discovery.

He ran as fast as he could. Farther, and farther. A half a mile, a mile. Jack refused to allow his legs and lungs to tire. And still farther he ran.

Then suddenly, Jack stopped dead in his tracks. He looked up at the Kingdom, then down at the ground, rubbed his eyes and looked up again.

Bewilderment filled his face, then anger.

"No! No!" he screamed, then fell to his knees.

He could never reach it! The Kingdom was not connected to the earth—it was floating high above in the sky.

This made no sense to Jack. He always thought of the Kingdom as a place where he would actually go.

"Well, what can I say?" Gnosis piped in again, polishing his fingernails on his jacket. "'I told you so' just doesn't even cover it. But Jack, now that you know the truth, let's go back and leave this horrendous place."

Covering his face with his hands, Jack groaned. "So I've traveled all this way to find a kingdom I can't enter." Dropping his hands, Jack's face was twisted in pain.

"Perception isn't everything," Azarel declared, suddenly appearing out of nowhere. "Jack, on this journey you have been learning that reality is not always what you see and touch. Have you not learned that faith is what unlocks the door to that which is truly real? Remember the Clouds of Despair? Remember the Forest of Stillness and the Raft of Freedom? Remember the Valley of the Shadow of Death, Jack?"

"Yes-s-s. But what does that have to do with it?"

"In each of these places, you discovered a different reality than what you physically saw at first glance. Walk with me." Azarel pulled Jack from his knees, and together they walked down the path.

"Jack, we have now come to the point in your journey where it is time for me to teach you about the ways of the Kingdom. In the beginning of this journey, I told you that you would need to gain more experience before any significant knowledge of the Kingdom would be relevant and helpful to you. You have gained the experience; now is the time for knowledge."

"Azarel, what good is a kingdom that can only be seen? Kingdoms are made to be lived in. The one hope that has kept me on this journey has been the belief that I could actually dwell in the Kingdom. But that's impossible! Just look at it! Look at the gulf between the Kingdom and the earth!"

"NO!" shouted Azarel as he threw his fist into the air and pointed his finger to the sky. "THERE IS NO GULF!"

Azarel paused and looked deeply into Jack's eyes. He then whispered, "The earth is imprisoned in the grid of deception—a false, illusory world of its own construction, to make humans believe in the gulf so that dwelling in the Kingdom is impossible."

Azarel's eyes glowed as passion stirred, his voice

crescendoed into overflowing exuberance.

"BUT NOT FOR LONG! THE DAY IS SOON COMING WHEN DECEPTION'S VEIL WILL FINALLY BE LIFTED!" he shouted.

The earth shook as Azarel thundered the divine declaration, "THE KINGDOM IS HERE! THE KINGDOM HAS COME!"

The words echoed in the air, stronger and stronger, filling every possible space in the atmosphere. Finally they ascended higher and higher as though returning to some other place from whence they had come.

After a few moments of silence, Azarel faced Jack. "Jack, the Kingdom used to be solely a heavenly reality, with only a few on the earth having access to it."

"What happened?"

"The fulfilled mission of the Son made it accessible to all who have the key of faith. The Father King brought forth the arrival of the Kingdom in a hidden, mysterious way while still not yet completely releasing it to the earth.

"On this journey, I said that you will come to know the Creator as Father King. Thus far you have been gaining knowledge of Him as Father. This is the key that centers you and gives you a sense of security. But the purpose you are seeking will not be found through that knowledge alone. You must also come to know Him as King. The Father is the King, and the King is the Father. You must know Him as both or you will never find the life that you seek. For that which you seek is found in the Kingdom, and the Kingdom is only found by those who know the King."

Azarel paused to let his words sink in.

"Jack, the Kingdom is not a destination you will

reach, nor an epoch you are awaiting as much as it is a reality you must now accept. It is a reality that transforms where you are right now. You access this reality by faith in the Son because the purpose of His coming was to usher in the Kingdom, and to release all the authority it provides. Like a seed, it is growing; like yeast, it is rising fuller and fuller. The Kingdom is here, and its fullness is hastened as you pray forth its coming. Jack, it was for this purpose that creation was made, and it is for this purpose that your heart beats.

"On this journey, you have learned much about your Thorn. But what you haven't learned is that your Thorn *marks you*. As you learn to embrace the Thorn that the Father has ordained for your journey, your embracing becomes your marking. The mark of the Thorn is the mark of the King—the mark of every true citizen of the Father King.

"Those with this humble mark have been granted the grace of vision—vision to see the truth through the eyes of faith while living in a world of deception. Yes, Jack, perception isn't everything. Don't let this heavenly hovering fool you. Its rule is intact and its rule now extends to you. Those who know not the Son shall not see nor know the rule of the King. The Kingdom remains invisible and its mystery remains incomprehensible; its ways shall ever remain offensive and scorned by those not marked by the King."

Jack shook his head in confusion.

"I don't understand. If the Kingdom is not a place to which I can go, then what is it I see in the sky? And why am I pursuing it?"

"What you see, Jack, is the *pattern* of Kingdom perfection now in heaven. It now hovers and awaits its full releasing. What you see is the full measure of the

Kingdom. Those who learn its ways learn to most fully access its authority. You don't go to it as much as *it comes to you*. What you see is the Son's declaration of the Father's provision that all authority is given to those who believe—authority to enforce and extend the Kingdom.

"You are pursuing it because that is what you were made for. All who stay on the Pathway of Faith draw nearer to its fullness. Jack, there is coming a day, and even now is, when the true sons and daughters of the Father King lay hold of unprecedented levels of Kingdom authority. They shall see the kingdoms of this world swallowed up by the Kingdom of the Father, and then the two shall finally be one!"

Jack replied, "But how do I accept this reality and access the rule of the King with such a great expanse between us?"

"Let's walk, and I will explain. It is time that you learn to recognize the doorways," motioned Azarel as they continued down the path.

Chapter Thirteen

THE DOORWAYS TO THE KINGDOM

The two travelers continued to hike along the pathway. Ahead of them, far in the distance, the meadows ended and woodlands began.

"Jack, the rules and ways of this realm are different from those of the earth. Though the Kingdom hovers above mankind, its habitation is brought down when its ways are lived out. Its community is expressed, its authority is released, and its boundaries are extended one way and one way alone—when the Doorways of Opportunity are recognized and entered."

"What do you mean, 'Doorways of Opportunity?'"

"Here in the earthly region are found doorways or portals to the Kingdom. These doorways connect the two realms and release the power of the Kingdom to its citizens below who know how to access it by giving themselves to its rules and its ways. Although the citizens of the Kingdom live *on* the earth, they are not *of* the earth. The reality of the Kingdom is a spiritual reality; but that spiritual reality does invade the physical reality in which you now live. Thus, we come to the need for doorways."

"Yes, the doorways..." repeated Jack.

"Though hard to spot, they are strategically scattered and always accessible, yet too often missed because of their small size. When the citizens of the Kingdom need authority in a situation, they are always given a doorway through which to access it. Whatever is needed, its provision is released through these obscure portals.

"Until the day when the earth's present age and heaven's eternal age become one, the enemy of the Father King remains busy at work. He continually throws obstacles in front of these doorways, seeking to halt the progress of the Kingdom."

Azarel turned to Jack. "Have you learned yet that you have an enemy?"

"Have I learned that I have an enemy? I've found many enemies on this trip!" Jack kicked a stone far off to the left of the path. "I wish I understood their ways so I could better defend myself against their tactics," he continued. "Somehow they keep tripping me up."

"So you have a need?"

"What do you mean?"

"It sounds to me like you are asking for wisdom, are you not?"

"Well, yeah. I guess you could say that's what I need."

"Then a doorway is provided. With every need, there is always a doorway. Humble yourself, and the door will be clear to you. Do you see it yet?"

"See what?"

"The doorway, Jack. Do you see the doorway?"

Jack had been so consumed in his conversation with Azarel that he hadn't even recognized they were now deep into the woodlands. He looked at the pathway outstretched before him with ferns, weeds, scattered rocks, and grassy patches lining its edges. There was a winding stream ahead of him flowing down the hill. He looked over at the rocky ledge dropping off to his right and then to the wooded hills rising up above him on his left.

"No. All I see are hills, trees, and rocks, and all these ferns and weeds growing up around them."

"What kind of rocks?"

"Some scattered. I do see an unusually placed mound of rocks over there, but there's no doorway anywhere."

"Humble yourself, Jack."

"Humble myself? What does my attitude have to do with anything?"

"To see the doorway, you must put yourself in a humble position."

"You mean...?"

"Yes."

Shrugging his shoulders in disbelief, Jack finally decided to comply with Azarel's implied suggestion and sank to his knees.

"Now, look," Azarel instructed.

Jack looked at the mound of rocks once again, only now from a lower perspective, and exclaimed, "Wow! How could I have missed that?"

"Much is missed from the neglect of one's knees."

"A cave! I couldn't see it before. I only saw the big rocks that shielded the entrance. What do I do now?"

"Enter."

When Jack and Azarel reached the mound of rocks set against the side of the steep hill, they got down on their hands and knees and crawled underneath several fallen tree trunks until they reached a small opening in the rocks.

"Go in. I know it's too dark to see much, but just go in."

Cautiously proceeding in the darkness, Jack and Azarel crawled about 50 feet into the cave when the tunnel began to open up both around and above them so they could stand up.

"Light," declared Azarel.

Instantly a blazing fire ignited inside a round border of rocks and gloriously lit up the darkness with a golden-like flame. On either side of the fire were two larger rocks.

"You need wisdom, and I will give it. Have a seat," motioned Azarel, as he pointed to one of the rocks. Staring across the dancing fire into Azarel 's serious face, Jack was mystified. Not unlike his time in the raft, there was some kind of unveiling happening inside this cave. It seemed as though he was beginning to see with the eyes of faith so that heaven's perspective was easier to lay hold of. Warm love and intense joy were welling up within him, something far deeper than any words could express. Tears slowly began to trickle down his cheeks.

It appeared as though the fire was somehow fueled by Azarel himself. Every few seconds, flashes of fire seemed to be exchanged between Azarel and the campfire on the ground. As he breathed in and out, the fire expanded and constricted as though it were an extension of his lungs.

The walls drank in the light until they dripped with a glorious luminescence and became a wonderfully brilliant canvas covered with a myriad of colors.

What was once merely a grungy cave of dirt, dust, and mud was transformed into a sanctuary of holy light, reflecting the glory and playing its part in a symphony of praise.

Jack began to softly weep. No longer could he contain the awe he felt.

"Jack, you are experiencing the light of the King. Most people never see it in such a concentrated and pure way. His light is truth, and in the presence of such light, all that is created breaks free from the bondage of decay and sings forth the song of worship. In such light, all things are released into their ultimate purpose—worship of the One who has created them.

"It is essential that you learn to live in the light—that is where the King's presence remains. It is too bright for you right now, but in time you will be able handle its intensity."

Azarel raised his hand, and the intensity of glory faded.

"You have learned to always look only at the obvious, Jack. Learn now to look for the hidden. The doorways are not always immediately revealed. At times you must persevere and endure, but a doorway is always given before it's too late. Through these doorways, faith is laid hold of and heaven's provision is released. Yet, none of this is released, Jack, if you don't find the doorways."

"Why is it so hard to find these doorways, Azarel?"

"Listen to me, Jack, and I will teach you about your enemy who desires to keep you away from the doorways. I believe your journey has led you to the point where you are now able to understand the dark side of spiritual reality. Dealing with him will be your next step."

Azarel was quiet for a moment. "There is an enemy who wants to keep you disconnected from the Kingdom of the Father. In that way, you will pose no threat to the advancement of his dark kingdom because you are only a bystander and not a participant.

"You have met the enemy on this trip, and he has taken many forms. You met him first in the realm of your thoughts in the Clouds of Despair; then you met him again in the Forest of Stillness as the dragon, then as Solus, and once again in the raft. When you know your enemy, you will understand his tactics.

"At one time, he lived in the heavens, but now dwells in the atmosphere of earth's air, ever seeking residence in the realm of humanity's mind through his agents of deception. In fact, he is known as the Prince of Lies or the Master of Deception."

Looking puzzled, Jack asked, "Do you mean he lives in my mind?"

"Well, it is through the doorway of your mind that he attempts to extend his influence. He seeks to enter the world of your thoughts where he attempts to gain your agreement with his lies and deceptions to fool you into believing that his ways are truth. By such deception, he attempts to derail you from finding the Doorways of Opportunity that release the provisions you need. The doorways are so obscure that only those whose minds have been filled with the light of the Kingdom have the clarity of thought to see these hidden portals. Your enemy will do all he can to darken your mind with deception. That is the reason you must learn to live in the light."

"How do I live in the light?"

"Obedience. Obedience releases light. You must do exactly as the King says. You will learn more of this later. Your challenge now is to learn the skill of discernment."

"How can I know whether the thoughts are mine alone, the Father King's, or the enemy's?"

"You must learn to recognize the Father King's voice of truth amidst all the enemy's voices vying for your attention. So many people assume that what is false has no power over them. But that too is deception. What one gives attention to is what one is inevitably controlled by, whether false or true. The skill of discernment has mostly to do with the discipline of the eyes. As you fix your eyes on the truth, you will not be controlled by all the deceitful voices seeking to lead you astray. The truth is light and when one looks into the light, that which is dark and deceptive is seen for what it is. Know, Jack, it is the truth alone that sets you free."

Azarel paused to allow Jack to take in what he had just said.

Jack shook his head. "I am overwhelmed, Azarel. You are explaining another world to me—an entirely different one than I have ever known. I have been oblivious to this kingdom my entire life. Deception, truth, darkness, light, the world of thoughts... Even though my mind is spinning, I think I am beginning to see some new light."

"Let me explain further, Jack, and I think you'll better understand the ways of the enemy. If his agents find an entrance, their tactics are three-pronged. First, they seek to fool the host into accepting their thoughts as his own. In so doing, a significant level of trust is instantly gained. They seek to prove their deception is truth, and that evil is somehow good. These masters of deception can create all kinds of arguments to strengthen their believability. Jack, this is why it is so important that you learn to guard your gates. When you pay attention to these deceivers, you extend an invitation to them to roam randomly in your mind, free from the light of truth.

"The purpose of every thought is the birth of a specific action, and the accumulation of actions leads to the building of one's life. Although the mind maintains the power of choice, the mind that relies on its own light or reasoning will surely fall to these masters of evil. You are no match for the darkness of these deceivers.

"Once the breach has been made into the mind, the second part of their attack is to infiltrate with many other agents—each one carrying its own building material for the construction of a fortress. Soon a stronghold against truth has been established with each stone in its walls a rebellious argument against the truth of the Kingdom.

"The final step begins when enough agents of the kingdom of darkness have gathered in the fortress to make a full scale invasion. At this point, they will quickly overcome the host and make him their slave. How tragic is the toll of these false arguments on the identity of the slave whose understanding has been darkened. The host is so deceived that he accepts his position of slave as normal. Discernment becomes impossible when truth has been rejected and deception has been admitted in its place.

"When truth has been veiled and a life of constructed reality has been put into place and its flag raised on high, the host comes to accept the darkness of the fortress as the world in which he lives.

"But," emphasized Azarel, with a rising smile on his face, "the invaders of a kingdom can be driven out and the reins of control can be taken back. How? By one way alone—the power of refusal. However, this can only be accomplished when the truth is seen and its light freely shines. In that brilliance, every false argument is demolished and every deceptive wall comes crashing down. Slavery is seen for what it really is, and freedom is cherished. Faith is unlocked, and destiny is released, when deception is silenced. Such is the nature of truth. In the presence of truth, deception cannot stand—it must flee because darkness cannot exist in the presence of light."

At this point, Professor Gnosis appeared on Jack's shoulder.

"Come now, Jack. This is all double-talk. You are in control of your mind—no one else. I think maybe we ought to get back soon so you can continue with your studies. That's the best way to know that you have not been deceived."

Maskon popped out on Jack's other shoulder. "You're free, Jack. You can do whatever you want to. You're capable of making quality decisions—you're an adult for heaven sakes. Just smile at whatever this guy is telling you and let's be on our way. There's lots of things for us to do."

Jack became irritated at his two shoulder companions. "Stop it, right now. I want to hear what Azarel has to say!"

Poof! Gnosis and Maskon were gone.

"Go on, Azarel. What were you saying? How do I get control?"

Azarel smiled and continued, "It will require a drive

of determination and a relentless press of persistence that the host has likely never before exerted. You must persist in believing the truth even when the looming evidence of circumstance and the flood of emotions you are experiencing seem contrary. You cannot rely on the power of reason either, since at this time, the mind would have been invaded and the fortress of darkness already built there.

"Jack, the road to freedom is the Way of the Thorn. You gain experience, freedom, and deliverance in the embracing of your Thorn. The knowledge of one's Thorn is the knowledge of one's inability to break free of the enemy's grip of deception, and this is the key that unlocks the grace that shatters these shackles of bondage. The King releases His authority to those who are not self-reliant, but to those who are humble, broken, and God-reliant. He always empowers those who are desperate enough to cry out for His help. Such ones are branded—they carry the mark of the Thorn.

"Freedom always comes with the price of dying to self-reliance and pride. Deception is broken by laying hold of the truth and imploring its light and power to come forth. Where the eyes of the mind allowed entrance to these impostors, so too by the eyes of faith are they expelled and light comes in. Reasoning is restored as discernment is realized from the releasing of that light.

"Remember, Jack, your eyes and ears are gates to the mind, so guard them well. The thoughts of the mind release the authority of kingdoms. That to which you give attention will ultimately rule you."

Azarel rose from his rocky stool, "Come now, Jack. It is time for us to move on."

As Azarel spoke, the light from the campfire shot up from the ground and surrounded him in a glow and radiated out into every corner and crevice of the cavern. Even the walls glowed from the reflecting effect of his light. Crawling out of the cave in the direction they had entered, Azarel said, "See Jack, the Father has provided. The Kingdom's provision was released when you found the doorway and entered it. Remember this lesson."

Emerging from the cave, Azarel's light rose like a mist from his body and suddenly shot forth over the trees to merge with the brilliance of the hovering Kingdom off in the distance.

Azarel put his hand on Jack's shoulder. "I am going to leave you again. You have to rely on what I have been teaching you. Do you now better understand how the enemies of the King take His sons and daughters as slaves?"

Jack drew himself up to his full height and spoke confidently, "Thoughts. He enters our lives by the gates of our eyes and ears. He enters into the world of our minds by pretending to be a thought of our own making when in fact he is a thought of deception. Once he gains agreement with the host as to the 'validity' of his lie, he quickly extends his authority in the life of the victim, making the host a captive to the power of deceptive thinking."

"You have learned well."

Swatting the side of his head, Jack said, "I see how false thinking has caused me much bondage. If only I could have rejected those lies from the beginning."

Shaking his head, Azarel replied, "You couldn't have, Jack—at least not on your own. These deceivers are such masters of disguise that, unless viewed next to truth, they will not be perceived as false. The one thing you must be sure to do is never take your eyes off the light. As long as you face the light, you will find the way to the Kingdom. Nothing else matters but facing the light.

"Jack, now that you understand the way your enemy works, it's time for you to begin to take a stand against him in your life."

"You can bet I want to Azarel, but how do I begin?"

"You must learn how to take every thought that enters your mind into the place of captivity by obeying the light, by looking at the light, and by ruthlessly following after the light, no matter what. This is the way to the Kingdom; this is the way into the authority of the Father King's realm. It's time you learn to walk past the voices."

"Walk past the voices?" Jack's head cocked and his forehead wrinkled. "What do you mean?"

"Stay on the pathway, Jack—follow the light!"

Suddenly with a loud explosion, a burst of light ripped through the atmosphere.

Azarel spun around and pointed up to a glow of light pulsating from the hovering Kingdom.

"Go Jack! Follow the light! Find the Kingdom!"

As Azarel was speaking, a powerful gust suddenly blew over them both. A swirling mass of wind enveloped Azarel in a massive flame that exploded upward and disappeared into the distant Kingdom.

Where once Azarel stood, now only the empty Pathway of Faith remained beckoning to Jack.

Jack was awestruck once again at the mystery and wonder of Azarel. He could clearly sense the Father's presence as he looked into the magnificent light emanating far above and through the terrain of the forested woodland.

But what's next? Jack wondered.

Chapter Fourteen

WALKING PAST THE VOICES

Jack straightened his shoulders and resolutely began down the path. The closer he drew to the Kingdom, the more brilliant was its light. When Jack focused his eyes on it, he was surprised that the glowing light did not hurt his eyes or blind his vision as the sun would. The more he looked at it, the clearer his mind and vision became.

Follow the light. Don't turn away. Follow the light. Don't turn away, repeated Jack to himself as he walked up the densely wooded and hilly terrain. Despite the thick forest, the light was always visible. After several miles of slow ascent, focusing on the light began to require a tremendous amount of his attention. Fatigue began to flood in, along with increased resentment over Azarel 's last command. It seemed to require such an exorbitant amount of attention that Jack decided not to be so rigid in following it. He reasoned that as long as he was aware of where the light was, he didn't need to keep diverting his attention away from the path. With a hint of irritation in his gait, Jack hiked on.

Thorn's throb now faintly began to coincide with Azarel 's words echoing in the air. "Guard your thoughts, Jack!"

The creeping darkness slowly began to prey on him. Jack's mind became cloudy and confused, and little thoughts began to irritate him.

The characters suddenly were all over him again.

"You need to save your energy, Jack. Stop looking up all the time. I tell you, you're wasting energy," said Professor Gnosis, arms folded, tapping his foot on Jack's shoulder.

Cleavon jumped and landed square in the middle of Jack's stomach. "Azarel doesn't trust you, Jack, even though you've trusted him completely. So he puts these ridiculous requirements on you. Just keep your eyes on the path and follow it. Remember, those were your instructions in the very beginning. How hard can that be?"

From somewhere deep inside, offense arose in Jack. *Azarel must be paranoid not to trust me to stay on the path. I would be stupid to get off it. I've learned that lesson. It's so broad I'll be fine as long as I keep my eyes on it. How hard can that be*?

Faintly flashing through his mind again were Azarel's last words: "Keep your eyes on the light, Jack. Look at the light."

An uneasy shudder washed over Jack—he shrugged it off, exhaled, and quickened his pace. Jack's body now bent slightly to his right as Thorn's warning continued its work, but he grit his teeth and pushed on.

Maskon whispered, "Jack, trust yourself. Look how far you've come on this journey. If anyone has ever proved himself trustworthy, it is certainly you."

Agreeing, Jack added his own thoughts, *I've come a long way. I'm so much closer to the Kingdom than I ever was. I'll never go back to the way I used to be. I can't believe how much I've changed.*

An unusual darkness began to quickly descend, and his vision grew cloudy, though he ignored it. Darkness grew and grew.

Thud! Splat! Jack tripped over a rock he hadn't seen and landed on another one that jabbed his side, right in the middle of Thorn's wound. Putting his hand on the spot, he could feel the wetness of his shirt from the blood beginning to flow.

He struggled up and sudden realized how dark it had become. Looking around, he tried to find the path.

I must have gotten off it somehow. I'll retrace my steps. Maybe I'll go this... Auuggg! moaned Jack as he pressed his hand over his wound, feeling Thorn's piercing.

Back a few paces, forward a few more, and then to the left. By now it was almost too dark to see anything.

"Oh no, oh no," echoed Jack in unison with Phobion's cries as he was shaking on his shoulder.

How could I have gotten so turned around?

Flashing through his mind, the words of Azarel gripped his attention: "The light of self is no match for the darkness of deception."

All the impish voices rose up in a loud chaotic roar, each one uttering their own foolish thoughts. Like puppets, they were totally controlled by the agents of darkness who spoke their lies directly into their ears

All the voices around him were screaming for Jack's attention. Nothing was clear; nothing made sense. He was now completely lost. Realizing his error, Jack immediately dropped to his knees in remorse and called out for help and waited.

The voices around him continued to rise.

"Jack, you've got to get us out of here! What are we going to do?" Phobion whimpered.

Anger and faith rose up in Jack. "Quiet! Enough!"

Instant silence. Peace descended when the four characters departed. Thorn's pain became slightly more manageable.

Jack took another look around him, and to his surprise, he saw a building off to his right and headed towards it.

It was a small one-room, A-framed building, with a steeple and cross on the roof. He looked above the door and saw the words, "Chapel of Alignment" carved into the dark wooden door frame.

What's that supposed to mean?

He read it again, and then a third time. The words seemed to echo in his soul, and began to stir within him a desire to worship God.

He pushed down the large wooden lever and entered the chapel. The room was so small that Jack was toe to toe with the altar in just five steps.

Immediately catching his eye was a sign hanging above the altar in front of him, which read:

Worship is a fire,
And devoted love is light—
Releasing heaven's resources
When pouring out one's soul.

He knelt. Suddenly it seemed as though heaven unloaded its atmosphere into the chapel. Thorn's pain instantly left as Jack began to feel a warm fluttering inside his stomach, which spread upward to his head and flowed down to his feet. Joy, peace, adoration, reverence, praise, and love began to bubble up from within his soul. Tears trickled, then streamed down his face as he clumsily tried to verbalize the extent of his love for his Creator and express a holy yearning to know Him more. Words spoken, words sung, words chanted—worship now exploded from his heart.

As he poured forth his praise, the darkness was broken. Something in that act had restored Jack's vision and reset his spiritual "compass." He now was certain of how to proceed; worship had realigned his mind and heart with his Creator.

After spending precious hours there in holy communion, Jack prepared to leave. As he opened the door, a stream of light flooded the room. Jack was amazed at the degree his eyes had been dulled by the darkness prior to entering the chapel. Now he could clearly see the light that he had lost sight of before.

"Such is the effect of truth, Jack," Azarel said, now appearing in the midst of the light.

"Deception's agents almost conquered you. If you had refused to listen to the desperation the Father was birthing in your heart through the prodding of your Thorn, and if you had not entered the chapel, you would still be stumbling around in the darkness. Whenever the light is consciously ignored through disobedience, darkness gains admittance into the mind of man."

"But I followed you all this way, Azarel. How could I be led astray after following you so far?"

"Jack, your focus must never be on how far you have come, but on how much you must trust. Looking back blurs your perception because your focus then is on yourself. Looking forward is what matters—for in that glance one sees how utterly impossible the journey ahead is. One cannot do it in one's own power. The forward glance releases the cry of desperation and the gaze of trust; this alone is what keeps the pilgrim safely on course. Perhaps the greatest undoing of so many sons and daughters of the Father King is a confidence and pride in how far they have come and in how much they have done, however slight or great it might be. Such vices never come when one's gaze is forward, but only when it is backward. It is a deceptive hope. The source of your hope must always be in the Father King and never yourself. When this focus is lost, your direction is lost as well."

Jack was pale and silent, stunned at his vulnerability. He dropped to his knees fearfully shaking, "I am paralyzed by truth, Azarel. How can I continue with such entrenched tendencies of self-deception? I thought I was safe, yet I was nearly a slave once again."

Azarel walked over to him and put his hand on Jack's head, "The awareness of your vulnerability is a result of your Thorn—this too is the Prod of God. Your Thorn must be viewed as a warning alarm. If your Thorn only results in guilt over your condition, then you have missed its very purpose. The aim of your Thorn is to get your attention, Jack, and focus your eyes and thoughts on the Father King and on Him alone.

"The Son has spoken the promise of a peace that passes all understanding for those who choose not to lean on their own reasonings but instead remember to acknowledge the Father in all that they do. Such peace, or lack thereof, the Father King has provided as a barometer for hearts and minds to be prodded into correct thought and focus. Let the release of peace stir you into the place of greater worship, and let its lack remind you of your need to press into that place of sacrificial praise—that is where you are safe, and that is where you will conquer."

Peace began to settle on Jack and he nodded in agreement.

"Jack, the truth you have just witnessed is the unveiled reality of the hopelessness of mankind's efforts toward freedom and life outside the realm of the Father King's Kingdom. You have now seen such hopelessness, but you are not consigned to its grip as long as you remember the light toward which you must gaze. On this side of heaven, you were created, more than anything else, to be a gazer at the light and a worshiper of the Father King. When you live for this purpose, everything else falls rightly into place, and peace will accompany all of your steps."

Every bit of fear vanished as Jack listened to the life-giving words of Azarel. The four characters were nowhere to be seen. Refreshment and peace flooded through every space of his body and soul!

Jack stood up, and together he and Azarel continued on their journey toward the Kingdom.

Chapter Fifteen

THE EYE OF THE THORN

As they traveled, Azarel described the Kingdom to Jack as a brand new mindset which, when engaged, becomes a whole new world in which one lives.

"Yes, it certainly is," said Jack, "a world within a world. But I'm still confused. You said it isn't a place of destination as much as a place released to me, yet you also said that the pursuit of it is also part of my purpose. I don't understand. I just want to get there."

Azarel stopped walking right at the edge of a sharp bend around a protruding cliff and looked at Jack. "You have been learning to access moments and periods of living in the Kingdom. Yet, the moment you stop pursuing the Kingdom is the moment you turn away from it. This side of heaven you are called, not merely to find it, but to never stop pursuing it. It is only in this way that you gain continual access.

"Jack, it is by faith that you are learning about and experiencing the Kingdom—but it is the Thorn that enables you to dwell there."

"Yes, it is a reminder of my brokenness."

"Yes, and by this brokenness you are empowered to break free from the power of the kingdoms of this world. Anything less is pride—and only humility can dwell inside the gates of the Kingdom."

Walking forward, Azarel pointed ahead. "Come, Jack, look and see what I mean. This is the doorway that will take you right to the gates of the Kingdom."

Around the bend, about 50 yards ahead, the Pathway of Faith abruptly stopped at the foot of a mountain out of which a large golden thorn appeared to protrude.

"Wow! What is that? It's so huge… it looks like a… a giant thorn."

"It is the doorway, Jack."

"Doorway? What do you mean? No one can walk through that!"

Cleavon started thumping on Jack's leg. "Not through that, Jack. That's no place for us to go."

Phobion hid his head under Jack's arm and said, "Nooooo, Jack. I'm so afraid something bad is going to happen!"

Cleavon jumped up to Phobion and they held onto each other, trembling all over.

Azarel began to explain, "With man it is impossible, Jack, but with God all things are possible. You must believe. The point of the thorn is the Gateway to Life—through this door one must pass the Test of the Wind and the Fire."

"Wind?" Cleavon shouted.

"Fire?" Phobion whimpered. "I knew something awful was going to happen!"

Azarel spoke louder, drowning out the two shaking characters, "Everything that is not truly you—the 'you' that the Father King made you to be—all of this will be consumed, burned, and driven away. Only those who believe can survive this test."

"Believe what?"

"Believe that the Father King is good, true, and trustworthy, that His ways are unsearchable, truer than even the way of understanding."

Suddenly the earth beneath them began to rumble and shake, and with a loud crack, lightning split the ground open in front of the travelers, igniting the chasm with shooting flames of fire from its sides as far down as either one could see. On the other side, the brilliant golden thorn was pointing right at Jack.

"Jump!" came a voice from heaven. Jack knew at once this was the voice of the Father King.

"Don't be crazy, Jack. You'll never make it alive," Phobion sobbed and began pulling on his pants leg. "Jack, I am soooo scared! Let's get out of here, now!"

A violent wind began to blow over Jack, and in its fury was heard a mass of aerial voices earnestly imploring:

Jump in the Wind!
Leap in the Fire!
Fall into Life!

Five times they pleaded their chorus. Then the wind stilled and the voices ceased.

"Jack, this is your last test before you enter the Kingdom. This jump will lead you to your final doorway. The Father King wants to bring an end to that which has caused you ongoing hindrance to Kingdom access.

"Don't walk by understanding. Walk by faith. You

don't see it now, but you will understand later. The needed understanding and light is available only after obedience. Obedience releases light."

All of the characters were at their posts screaming.

Maskon was the loudest. "Jack, resist Azarel. You don't need him. Walk away and get out of here now!"

Phobion and Cleavon were still holding onto each other sobbing. Gnosis started to shake Jack. "Jack you know better than this. Resist Azarel and save yourself. You can walk away right now, and we can go back to your old life. We can study all about some of these principles and decide which ones we should follow." Getting more desperate, Professor Gnosis pleaded, "Now, Jack, you'll turn back now if you're as smart as I think you are!"

Their noise was almost deafening. Jack began to feel paralyzed with the terror of jumping into a sure death.

Jack raised his eyes and cried out, "Father King!"

As he did so, he glanced at the characters and saw only their mouths moving, but no noise coming out. In that same moment, Jack was filled with new faith and hope.

Trusting the sovereignty of Azarel's voice more than the terror before him, Jack filled his lungs with air and with a loud yell took a giant leap.

He fell...deeper and deeper into the heart of the earth. In the midst of his fall, a very unusual thing began to happen. The force of the wind pounded over Jack's body while at the same time the flames shooting out of the sides of the chasm lapped over him. In an unusual way, the combination of the heat was balanced with the cooling of the wind so that he wasn't even slightly burned.

Though Jack wasn't physically consumed in the

flames, he underwent another kind of consuming—more precisely, a peeling.

Like skins of an onion, layers of Jack began to burn off him and blow away into the Chasm of Forgetfulness—where all that needs to be discarded is removed and thrown away, never to be remembered again.

Each layer was a kind of mask or, most specifically, a way of non-authentic living. With each shedding of these "false selves" came explosions of light followed by bursting sensations of freedom.

No longer could the characters choose to stay hidden—they popped up once again all over Jack, holding on for dear life.

Trembling like a leaf, Maskon was the first to be torn away from Jack by the wind. In the wind came a voice saying, "Jack, no longer shall you pretend to be something you are not, no longer shall you worry about being perfect; integrity and contentment will be your mark." And Maskon disintegrated into a swirling stream of dust.

Phobion was the next to go. He trembled so much that he couldn't hold onto Jack any longer—first one hand then the other was pried loose by the violent wind and he, too, was torn away. And the voice said, "Jack, no longer will you be ruled by your fears, but peace will be your mark."

Professor Gnosis was desperately trying to find something in his notebook that would save him, but because he was using his strength to flip the pages, the wind was easily able to pry him from Jack, and he, too, disintegrated into the maelstrom. And the voice said, "Jack, your pride has been dealt with along the way, so you will no longer be ruled by it; rather, humility shall be your mark."

Cleavon was the last to go because of his many suction cups that plastered him tightly onto Jack. Finally, the heat of the fire was so intense that it made his cups slide off and soon he, too, became dust blowing in the wind. "Jack, be whole! No longer will you live for the creation, but the Creator. The life that you seek will be found in the place of devotion to My love."

Jack was free! Never before had he felt so free. He was free to fully be himself while no longer shackled by any fear.

Although Jack continued to fall, he felt no fear. At last he felt clean and more alive than ever before! Still falling, Jack began to assume that all the corrupted layers had been stripped away.

Still he fell farther and farther until he began to feel self-conscious—naked, exposed, and vulnerable. A current of wind as sharp as a knife suddenly slit his back between his shoulders, rushed through his body and exited out of his feet, hands, legs, and sides.

This time the wind was not peeling something *off* of Jack, it was cutting something *out* of his very core, which had an entrenched root system.

Jack was undergoing a cutting of the core of self-concern, which caused him to hold onto his life and try to control it. This was the one part of him that was always so resistant to faith. Like a surgeon's knife dealing with a cancerous tumor, the wind skillfully cut deep into Jack's gut. The sounds of ripping and tearing filled the air as the core was cut out, but it was still attached by its deep root system fastened into Jack's soul. The harsh fire and persistent wind pounded down upon it until slowly but surely the roots began to give way.

At last the wind rushing around the core and

through the roots released a high pitched sound eventually becoming a soul-curdling scream: "M-E-E-E-E!" and the selfish cancer was finally torn out. As the core was discarded into the Chasm of Forgetfulness, Jack could see that the ends of its roots culminated in the form of hands grasping the air as they were blown away.

Jack was almost blinded by the sudden release of light now exploding around him. Instantly he was encompassed in a pair of massive hands which lifted him back up and out of the chasm and on the other side where the massive thorn had stood.

It was quickly evident to Jack that the wind and the fire had changed him. With every shedding and stripping of skin and the departure of the creatures that were now no longer a part of him, his perspective and vision had totally changed. The object before him was nothing like the giant thorn he had last seen.

What previously appeared as a protruding thorn had somehow become a doorway—the glowing entrance to a cave. Whether the thorn had literally changed or whether Jack's perception of it had changed, he didn't know. But now, the magnificent entrance was beautifully ornamented beyond Jack's wildest imaginations.

Azarel appeared in front of the entrance. "Congratulations, Jack! You have survived the fire and the wind and the fall. You see how the thorn has become the doorway! The change you have undergone is as drastic as the difference in the appearance of the thorn. You now stand stripped down—simple and true. You are living in the realm of unselfishness and true humility. Such a posture releases the perspective and vision of heaven so that you can see things, not as they seem to be, but as they really are. Let's enter."

"Azarel, all I saw before was the point of the thorn—

I was completely blind to the doorway in the midst of it."

"Jack, such are the doorways of the Kingdom; they are always there, we just don't always see them. On the other side of the Thorn, if it's humbly embraced, is the Kingdom. Jack, you already went through the thorn's point when you submitted to the wind and the fire. Since the Thorn has already done its work in you, your eyes no longer focus on it. Instead, they see the glorious doorway.

"Only that which is pure can enter the Kingdom—anything less will never survive. The cancerous effects of the dark kingdoms of this world have so defiled mankind that it cannot even see its own evil. No man or woman can enter the Kingdom unless he or she is drastically changed.

"Truth alone has the power to reveal and the power to heal. Such truth never comes without a cost—and the cost is always the Thorn. So the 'miserable' Thorn, when humbly embraced, is always the precious doorway to transformation. Yes, the King has ordained that the painful Thorn is also the healing Thorn—by it, the vices of mankind are exchanged for the virtues of heaven. Never despise your Thorn, Jack!" Azarel smiled as they walked into the brilliantly lit cavern.

They proceeded through the arched doorway, splendidly ornamented with nuggets of gold and silver and clusters of diamonds. Inside everything was fashioned of pure gold—the ground, the walls, and the ceiling. Embedded in the walls were jewels and gems of incredible variety. Light reflecting through these stones and off the gold walls created the image of woven bands and streams of rainbow colored lights throughout the room.

As Jack scanned the room, he noticed that there

were nine predominant gems grouped in various sections of the cave's walls: diamonds, emeralds, rubies, topaz, sapphire, amethyst, pearls, garnets, and jasper. As Jack looked closer, he saw that carved into the wall next to each one were one of the following nine words: Love, Joy, Peace, Patience, Kindness, Goodness, Faithfulness, Gentleness, and Self-control.

"What does this mean, Azarel?"

"These are the nine qualities of fruitful living in the Father's Kingdom. These qualities are more precious than the very stones on which they are written. The purpose of the gems is to represent the value of these qualities. Although they fall so short—these are the only earthly symbols that approach a representation of their costly value. Just as these words are carved and crafted into the walls of this cave, so too are these qualities carved and crafted by the knife of the Thorn into the lives of the Kingdom's inhabitants. As these qualities are brought forth into the lives of the saints, they too will shine and reflect the light of the King as do these golden walls and gems you see around you."

With a glazed over look on his face, Jack stared at the beautiful gems all around him. It was as though their beauty had hypnotized him. Grabbing Jack's arm, Azarel began to shake him.

"Listen, Jack. As beautiful as the cave is, its only purpose is to show you how much the Father King values the broken life. These stones are but a symbol of something much greater. If you stay too long in such a place you would become so enamored by them that you would miss the greater "jewels" they represent. Don't be content to merely settle for the symbol and miss the priceless reality of His Kingdom. Let us now proceed."

Azarel and Jack descended deeper and deeper into

the heart of the cave. Now the light emanated not only from Azarel but from Jack as well.

Initially, the pathway through the cave was extremely spacious—involving entire rooms of tremendous proportions, flashing with yet even more jewels in the walls. However, eventually it closed in tighter and tighter until the only remaining way was a dusty rocky tunnel. Through it, Jack and Azarel were forced to crawl on their hands and knees and then finally drag themselves along with their elbows and forearms.

"Azarel, are you sure we took the right tunnel?"

"I am certain, Jack. This side of heaven, transformation is a continual process. In the presence of such glorious light and wholeness, one can easily forget the necessity of maintaining an ongoing posture of humility. Jack, the Father King is posturing you for correct entry into the Kingdom. Look! Do you see the light ahead?"

Jack saw a dim light off in the distance.

"That is the exit, Jack. We are almost there!"

As they approached it, the light grew brighter and brighter until it became blinding. It poured over Jack as he groped his way forward with his eyes tightly closed. They finally reached the exit and crawled through some kind of tapestry or veil.

The light was so overwhelming that it even penetrated through his firmly shut eyelids until he finally collapsed, unconscious from its weight.

Azarel reached down and touched Jack's head, instantly restoring his strength and giving him the ability to open his eyes in spite of the brilliance. Standing up, Jack looked behind him. He could no longer see the cave, but he saw the filmy material he had just crawled through. He then gasped as he saw an alarming sight—

his body lay limp and lifeless on the ground on the other side of the veil. Within the span of only several feet hung the gulf of two entirely different worlds!

"How can this be? If I am here, how can I be there?" asked Jack pointing over at his body. "Where am I?"

"In Truth," Azarel said. "Self-focus is impossible to experience in this place."

"Your spirit has left your physical body because your body cannot stand in the presence of the Father King until the day He gives you a new and different kind of body. Until then, your physical body shuts down when you get this close to Him."

It was hard for Jack to say he was "seeing," because in this place, vision was much more than seeing—it also involved other abilities like sensing, being, and knowing. Here these qualities were experienced in their fullness. Vision was a combination of his eyes' ability to see and his spirit's ability to be. In this place, fullness of life was lived in every moment and in every circumstance because vision and being were so closely linked.

Jack's senses were quickly adjusting to this new place, and as a result his physical body, lying just a few feet from him, was beginning to fade away into a mist until eventually it vanished completely. As his senses were "unlearning" the way they used to operate, that which used to be seen according to the "old vision" began to disappear as his "new vision" began to take over.

"Where did I go?"

"You are still there. But in this place you quickly become unaware of yourself and are instead consumed with what you were made to experience. Look up!"

Jack looked up and with explosive joy screamed out,

"The Kingdom! I see the Kingdom! I finally made it to the Kingdom!"

"Jack, the Kingdom has always been present and, for some, even in your realm, it is visible. But it can only be seen by the eyes that have been freed from the power of selfish nature; and it can only be approached by those who have found its Doorways of Opportunity. You are now seeing what has always been, only now without the hindrances you've always known. Do not forget that it was the prodding of your Thorn that led you here."

Jack looked up at a sight more glorious than he could have ever imagined.

The Kingdom lay before him.

Chapter Sixteen

THE KINGDOM

The Kingdom was breathtaking. Its prominent feature was light—exploding from every square inch of its surface. Azarel began to tell Jack all of the specific dimensions and qualities of the Kingdom.

There was a massive wall over 200 feet thick surrounding the Kingdom. The walls consisted of 12 foundations, each adorned with its own type of precious stone. There were 12 gates, three on each of the four sides, each one fashioned from a single gigantic pearl. The city was laid out in a perfect cube. Its dimensions were staggering—over a thousand miles in each dimension of length, width, and height!

As they stood before the central gate on the north side of the Kingdom next to the Pathway of Faith, Jack recognized the River of Life, which now had become merely a gentle flowing stream. In front of the steps, the stream emptied into a narrow crevice and then dropped into a large channel with connecting tunnels that fed the water into the city and disbursed it. Jack kept shaking his head over the majesty of it all.

Azarel said, "You have now completed the Journey of Honest Reckoning, Jack. The Kingdom of the Father lies behind these doors. I have fulfilled what the Son has sent me to do. Just as I have been leading you in the knowledge of the Kingdom, now I will be leading you in the life of the Kingdom." Then he was gone, at least visibly.

Jack stood alone before the massive gates of the Kingdom—staring into the entrance he had been seeking his entire life. Yet, he still felt unprepared.

Having now learned well the posture of holy desperation, Jack dropped to his knees and began to pray.

"Father King, You have taught me a new way of living and have unveiled Your presence. You have stripped me down—and I am a new man! But I fear lest in a moment of weakness a doorway will be opened for darkness and deception to enter in once again and ruin the life I have found on this journey."

The gate slowly swung open, and through it flooded a stream of white radiance. Behind the light was a Person. Staring into the light, though practically blinded by its brightness, Jack knew exactly who it was—the Son.

The Son stepped through the gate and said "We have been expecting you, courageous one."

Jack dared not even to look up. He was embarrassed by such words.

"Stand up, Jack Avery."

Jack complied with the command.

The Son looked at Jack and asked, "What would you like Me to do?"

"I-I-I-I am afraid that I will have a problem with the four creatures who hung onto my life for so long, taunting my mind and harassing my heart. C-c-can You help me with this?" Jack asked.

"Only if you believe, Jack. In My Kingdom, faith is always the key that unlocks any door."

"I do believe."

The Son looked at Jack and commanded, "Take seven steps back."

Although puzzled, Jack immediately obeyed and stepped back seven times.

The Son looked at Jack and proclaimed, "From dust to dust was the old man. From spirit to spirit is the new. Remember what those four creatures became?"

"I guess they all turned into a swirling mass of dust."

Pointing at a mound of dust on the ground next to Jack, the Son then breathed on it and as it scattered in the air, a flaming heart arose, beating and pulsating, which steadied itself in front of Jack's heart.

The Son looked at Jack and said, "Receive your new heart, Jack Avery."

The flaming heart landed on Jack's chest and began to press itself into his own heart, lifting him off the ground. Jack began to vibrate until he dropped to the ground, as if he were dead.

As the Son stepped forward, reached down, and took Jack's hand to raise him up, he felt a surge of life run through him.

The Son then took His hand, plunged it in Jack's side, and pulled out a very large thorn.

"Jack, for every Thorn, if willfully accepted, there is a rose, and I am that Rose. I am your single treasure. Learn to embrace your Thorn, and you will learn to access My life and power at every point of need."

The Son closed His hand over the thorn and squeezed tightly until it began to drip with blood. He opened it to reveal a beautiful rose lying alongside the thorn.

"Jack, My blood transforms, and when the Way of the Thorn is embraced, it will lead to the Life of the Rose where the fragrance of divine grace makes all things new."

The Son then closed His hand over both the rose and the thorn and plunged His hand back into Jack's side, leaving them inside.

"I'm a new man! Thank You for giving me an entirely new life on this journey."

"You are indeed a new man. Now walk in My light and continue to put to death the deeds of the flesh. Your little characters have lost their power and hold on you, but they or others like them still must daily be resisted or they will return. Jack, this side of heaven, the Thorn remains because it is the Father's prod—leading and directing you in the way you should go, and reminding you of your power to choose. Otherwise, those unholy characters will surely take root once again even in this new heart.

"Through the new mindsets you've received from Azarel, you will be able to access the rule and authority of My Kingdom even when you are walking in a land of people who know nothing of My rule. The Kingdom goes where the King goes, and the King is present wherever His authority is enforced. Go and enforce My authority and be an extender of the boundaries of My Kingdom and an imparter of My life to all who remain captives in the kingdoms of this world. Go then and share this with others! Proclaim this freedom and release My light to all who don't see! Go and proclaim freedom to every one of them!"

Finishing these words, the Son stepped back through the gate and said, "Jack, you have now found the one thing you have searched for all your life. Now you can spend the rest of your life doing what you were created to do. Welcome home! Receive the Kingdom!"

Brilliant light erupted out of the Son's eyes, hands, and feet. He began to glow in a white light that grew brighter and brighter until it was too bright for Jack to look at. A wind began to blow and swirl into an increasingly stronger force around the Son, and He exploded into the form of an inexpressibly beautiful swirl of brilliant glory. The light and glory grew in size and moved backwards from the place where the Son initially stood, swirling around the entire Kingdom, causing it to glow brighter and brighter. Finally, completely consumed, the entire Kingdom was swept up into the air—spinning faster and faster, stronger and stronger, until the entire swirling mass was entirely swallowed up in the light.

The same light was exploding off Jack, and the wind pounded in his ears. The presence of the glory was overwhelming and the weight of the holy light and wind became too much for him to experience. As he was about to pass out, the swirling wind dipped down, pulled Jack's spirit up and into itself and then hovered over his physical body which had just become visible. In a split-second, the entire swirling mass darted right into his heart and disappeared.

Suddenly Jack was aware that he was flying through some kind of tunnel. He was moving incredibly fast until some trees came into view. Under them lay his body, and with a jolt it jerked all over. His eyelids twitched, then his eyes suddenly opened and his fingers began to move. He felt vibrantly alive as his spirit slammed into the reality of the physical world, his garment of flesh.

The words of the Son thundered through the atmosphere and found its echoed vibrations in Jack's heart, every syllable pounding in divine proclamation: "The Kingdom of God is within you!"

Jack looked up to where the Kingdom had been, only now there was no trace of it. But he firmly believed it was still there. Although it was invisible to his physical eyes, he could spiritually sense it. His believing was now his seeing. Jack was immediately struck with the realization that he was living in two worlds at the same time—he was living in the Kingdom of the Father King while at the same time living in the earthly world.

He heard the Son's words:

"Jack, you have completed this journey. You have learned the lessons reserved for it. It is now time for the spiritual eyes and ears of your heart to see and hear what has recently been unveiled to your physical eyes and ears. On the Journey of Honest Reckoning, you have received all that you need to live. The eyes and ears of your heart are where the realities of the Kingdom are seen and experienced."

As Jack lay there on his back, his vision suddenly became blurry, like when a person is underwater and looks up at the world above.

"Go!" the voice shot through his heart.

By the time Jack got up to his knees, his vision was perfectly clear. He was now back in the physical world he had left behind at the beginning of his journey.

He looked ahead to see the trail sign before him: Welcome to New Heights Trail.

Jack looked at his watch. 10:30 AM.

He had experienced a whole new world and found the Kingdom, while his physical life had never even skipped a single beat of its rhythm in time and space.

Such is life in the Kingdom—it is not bound by time or space but is found in the place of the spirit from which it affects and influences the world of the earth.

Jack headed toward the beginning of the trail where he saw his pack still lying on the ground where he had left it.

A huge smile slowly covered his face as he said, "I guess I won't be needing that. I've finally learned to trust my Provider!"

Jack Avery turned on his heels away from the trail. As he walked toward his car, he began to feel a familiar jab.

His hand gently touched his side, just under his heart.

And then he smiled.

"Thank you, God. Thank You for my Thorn."

FOR EVERY THORN THERE IS A ROSE

What is a thorn?
A nuisance, I say,
A nuisance.

And why a nuisance?
Because all I want is the lovely rose,
But when I seek to grab it
Into my hand the hidden dagger goes.

What is a rose?
Lovely the essence.
"Ah lovely"...
  to behold
    to smell
      to touch.
So give me the rose,
But the thorns...withhold.

There once was a man who had a thorn.
Upon him it struck
And to his dismay,
Remained permanently stuck.
To God three times he prayed
The awful nuisance to take away.

From heaven above the Lord looked down,
With tears in His eyes
And pain on His face.
There He cried, "Behold the Rose! Behold My Grace!
The thorn I'll not remove, for I love too much.

"Though it hurts I'll not remove it.
Only in that hurt… that soil
  of weakness
    of brokenness
Will the lovely Rose grow,
Will My grace bloom!"

We all love roses,
We all hate pain,
But for every thorn, there is a Rose.
I found a rose. I met the Rose...
Oh, so lovely Rose of Sharon.

I prayed, "Dear God, take away the thorns;
I only want the Rose—
I love roses,
But I hate pain."

"My child, My child, many desire the Rose,
For therein is life eternal
Fullness of living—
But the way of the Rose is the way of the thorn."

Many seek the Rose,
But at the testing of the thorn
  most
    fall
      away.

The testing of the thorn
Reveals the restless cravings of the heart.
Reject the Rose
For the carnal cravings of the heart

Or for the true craving of the heart
Accept the Rose!

"Child, child, love the Rose.
Embrace your thorn
As a faithful friend."

At the place of the thorn
Is the pain of restless need exposed.
Here is the test:
Wait for the Rose in the thorns of pain
Or run to a rogue rose with substitute solace.

At the testing of the thorn,
Divine grace turns my pain and tears
To peace and joy
Where all my need is swallowed up...

We all love roses,
We all hate pain,
But for every thorn, there is a Rose.
The choice is yours and the choice is mine;
On the journey to the Rose must every man born
Face the horrible testing of the thorn.

Face the pain.
Embrace the thorn.
Be embraced
By the Rose.

EPILOGUE

It has been my prayer that this story has shown something of what it means to be honest with ourselves and with God. Through such honesty I hope that we come to understand in a clearer way what it means to live in the grace of Christ. Just like Jack, may we throw all our inhibitions aside and jump into that glorious River of Life and be carried right to the doors of the Kingdom of God where we will finally enter into the life for which our hearts have so desperately yearned.

This side of heaven, Thorn's pain and wail will never cease—but if we persevere, our thorn will soon become our faithful friend, and there we'll see that the pain is the prod...God's loving poke keeping us moving and reminding us of our utter need for GRACE. And the Way of the Thorn shall be known as the pathway to our destiny!

> *Now faith is being sure of what we hope for and certain of what we do not see. This is what the ancients were commended for and why they admitted that they were aliens and strangers on earth. They were longing for a better country—a heavenly one. Therefore God is not ashamed to be called their God, for he has prepared a city for them* (Hebrews 11:1,13,16).

About the Author

David Trementozzi serves as the editor of *KAIROS* magazine, a publication of Eagles' Wings, a relational network of believers involved in global outreaches. David also serves as both the pastor of the Eagles' Wings team, and the director of the EW Internship Program.

David often speaks at various services, conferences, and meetings in the United States. David's ministry calls believers to deeper levels of authenticity and spiritual devotion in their pursuit of God. David has also written the book, *Holy Desperation: Devotional Poems for the Surrendered Soul.*

David and his wife Emily reside in Amherst, New York, where together they minister with Eagles' Wings.

David is available for speaking engagements. He can be reached at:

David Trementozzi
PO Box 450, Clarence, NY 14031
716-759-1058
davidtrementozzi@eagleswings.to
www.thewayofthethorn.com

OTHER BOOKS
FROM EVERGREEN PRESS

PALADINS, THE *Tim Stoner*
Four teenagers are whisked to another world where their lives are changed forever. Harry Potter, move over—these teens experience the *real* power!
ISBN 1-58169-002-9 352 p. PB $12.95

PARADIGM QUEST, THE *Jean Koberlein*
An allegory written in the style of *Hind's Feet on High Places*, it challenges you to reach higher and go further to find fresh vision and purpose and embark on your own Paradigm Quest.
ISBN 1-58169-052-5 176 p. PB $10.95 retail

BITS OF HEAVEN *Amy Lynn*
We are all surrounded by bits of heaven—tiny miracles that surround us. Here's a potpourri of compelling stories, each accompanied by an inspiring poem. Rediscover the infinite treasures that encapsulate our lives.
ISBN 1-58169-029-0 184 pg. PB $10.95

CATS IN THE PARSONAGE *Clair Shaffer, Jr.*
Warm and humorous stories of a country preacher's feline friends that not only refresh the soul but teach a few lessons along the way. Taffy and Tiffany will warm their way into your heart and tickle your funnybone. Any cat lover's must reading!
ISBN 1-58169-060-6 176 pg. PB $9.95

HEY BRUDDER DAN! (humor) *Dan Zydiak*
An aspiring writer turned church custodian got more than he bargained for when he took the job.
ISBN 1-58169-020-7 96 p. PB $6.95

EARTH BETWEEN, THE (fiction) G.B. *Chase*
A time machine with a "mind" of its own…events foretold by ancient prophesies captured on tape…covert terrorists preparing to infiltrate a sleepy, rural town. Better fasten your seatbelt! ISBN 1-58169-046-0 256 p. PB $10.95

LIGHT TEAM, THE *Jeff McNair*
Travel to the world of two suns and find truth in an unexpected way. You'll see how ordinary men join with a man called Iaman to become quite extraordinary.
ISBN 1-58169-005-3 192 pg. PB $9.95

SECRET WATERS — M.*J. Gardner*
A story set in 16th century England about a wealthy landowner who must defend his castle against the enemy. Good lessons on defending what the enemy wants to steal from you.
ISBN 1-58169-004-5 160 pg. PB $6.95

ADVENTURES AT THE GRANDPARENTS' HOUSE
Marge Alexander (Kid's fiction–middle readers)
Kids will want to read this over and over as they enjoy the adventures of Amos the Scarecrow and Phoebe the bunny. Along the way, lessons are learned and insights are shared in a way that captivates children.
ISBN 1-58169-064-9 96 pg. HC $9.95

All books available from your local bookstore, Amazon.com, BN.com, ChristianBook.com, or call 888-670-7463